'I want you, ...

She could sense h...
to admit his need...
was clearly an alien experience. What did he
mean by not being able to offer her what she
wanted? All she wanted—all she could feel at
that point was the desperate need for his touch.
To find out whether reality could possibly
match a much cherished memory.

'I want you, too,' was all she could say.

Alison Roberts was born in New Zealand and, she says, 'I lived in London and Washington D.C. as a child and began my working career as a primary-school teacher. A lifelong interest in medicine was fostered by my doctor and nurse parents, flatting with doctors and physiotherapists on leaving home, and marriage to a house surgeon who is now a consultant cardiologist. I have also worked as a cardiology technician and research assistant. My husband's medical career took us to Glasgow for two years, which was an ideal place and time to start my writing career. I now live in Christchurch, New Zealand, with my husband, daughter, and various pets.'

Recent titles by the same author:

MORE THAN
A MISTRESS

BY
ALISON ROBERTS

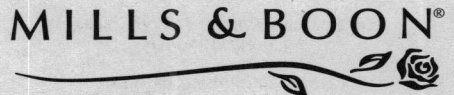

MILLS & BOON®

First published in Great Britain 1999
Harlequin Mills & Boon Limited,
Eton House, 18-24 Paradise Road, Richmond, Surrey TW9 1SR

© Alison Roberts 1999

ISBN 0 263 81717 2

Set in Times Roman 10½ on 12 pt.
03-9907-47799-D

Printed and bound in Spain
by Litografia Rosés, S.A., Barcelona

CHAPTER ONE

SMITH.

Anna Kessel underlined the name of the incoming patient in her notebook and then shoved it into the pocket of her white coat with an irritated sigh. It wasn't the patient's fault that the name now leapt out at her and gave her an unpleasant jolt every time. Such a common name—it was inevitable that it would crop up everywhere. It was *his* fault. Such an obvious alias! Mike Smith, indeed! Incredibly unoriginal. Surely he could have come up with something better than that?

What was even more irritating was the way Anna was failing to get over her preoccupation with the owner of the alias. Her holiday had been over more than a week now. Any normal person would have found the pressure and exhaustion she was struggling with more than enough to drive away the memory of a holiday fling.

Anna collected an IV tray from the supply room of Ward 26. Mrs Bell's IV line had tissued and needed to be replaced. Mr Ellison was unable to sleep due to inadequate post-operative pain relief and also needed to be seen. With a bit of luck nothing else urgent would turn up before the new admission arrived in the ward. Anna marched down the dimly lit central corridor of the ward. What was a seventy-four-year-old lady doing to break her hip at this time of night anyway? Was it all part of a plot to make the life of a newly fledged doctor virtually intolerable?

Anna's step slowed. It was hard to be rational at 3 a.m. She had never been more tired in her entire life. Even the thought that she'd recently had a holiday seemed like a remote fantasy. And as for what had happened....!

Mrs Bell was half-asleep. She roused as Anna applied a tourniquet to her upper arm and tightened it gently.

'I'm just going to replace your IV line, Mrs Bell,' Anna whispered. 'The other one has blocked so you're not getting the medication you need. It'll only take a minute.'

'I hope so,' her patient mumbled. 'I'm very tired.'

You and me, both, Anna thought. She also hoped the procedure would be quick. These things were all fine in theory but she had found out very rapidly that the practicality was something quite different. She could feel the vein perfectly well—a kind of squashy rope beneath the skin—but she knew that they had an uncanny tendency to move out of the way of an approaching needle. If you couldn't catch them by surprise the first time some also had the astonishing knack of instantly shrivelling and becoming impossible to locate by anything other than a lucky guess.

Anna held the tip of her tongue firmly between her teeth and made a decisive jab. She had already learned that the worst thing was to try and sneak carefully up on a vein. They were way too smart to fall for that approach.

'Got you!' Anna's triumphant whisper as the blood came easily back into the syringe made Mrs Bell's eyes open smartly.

'What did you say?'

'We're all done.' Anna flushed the IV line and disconnected the syringe. She deftly connected the tube dangling from the IV pole and reached up to turn the tiny plastic wheel to restart the drip. 'You can go back to sleep now, Mrs Bell.'

'I will, thank you, Doctor. You should get back to sleep yourself.'

'I should be so lucky,' Anna said wryly. She paused for a moment in the corridor, trying to remember in which direction Mr Ellison's room lay. Dimly lit and empty of the daytime congestion, the ward suddenly impressed Anna with its size. Tauranga Hospital was a large provincial centre and Orthopaedics had to be the most hectic specialty to have landed for her first three-month rotation. Several times in the last week Anna had asked herself whether this was what she wanted. The hard-won medical degree had seemed an end in itself. Even the hospital experience of her sixth year at medical school hadn't prepared her for the reality of initiating her career.

Any introduction would surely have been easier than Orthopaedics. There were two surgeons for the department and they each had their own registrar, but Anna had been dismayed to find she was the only house surgeon for the specialty. The head of department, Tim McPherson, had been apologetic but he'd been sure she would cope. A grey-haired, kindly man, approaching retirement, Tim McPherson specialised in joint replacement and geriatric patients of which there were more than he could handle alone. His fellow consultant was due back from holiday shortly and perhaps the pressure would ease a little then.

Mr McPherson's registrar was Ken Slater. Anna

liked Ken. He was a junior registrar in his second year and was working towards taking his Part 1 examinations on the road to becoming a consultant surgeon. Already preoccupied with the formidable exams to come at the end of the year, he still made time to try and make Anna feel at home and to ease her initial confusion.

'You'll need six pairs of hands and thirty-six hours in a day,' he told her helpfully. 'In the good old days there would have been a house surgeon for each registrar but I guess it was a nice, easy area for management to do a bit of cost-cutting. Have you been given a good résumé of your duties?'

'Oh, yes.' Anna couldn't help sighing. A senior registrar, Erica Savage, had spent an alarming hour informing her of her duties. Erica had passed all the examinations to become a fellow of the Royal Australasian College of Surgeons some years ago. Now in her mid-thirties, she was waiting to take up a consultant position, probably when Tim McPherson retired, though due to the ever-increasing workload and waiting lists there was pressure to increase the staff to three consultants. Erica was intelligent, ambitious and intimidatingly professional. Tailored clothing, short hair, wire-rimmed spectacles and a clipped tone that did not invite familiarity made Anna feel she hadn't graduated at all.

'You'll be responsible for admissions, taking histories, making initial physical examinations, planning initial diagnostic tests and documenting everything accurately.' The look Anna had received had implied that accurate reporting was not something Erica usually found up to scratch.

'You'll see your patients every day to update their

status and you'll have results available for consultant rounds.' Again Anna had felt that Erica hadn't been satisfied with her predecessor's abilities in this area.

'You can make changes to treatment with consultation or initiate emergency treatment if necessary. You'll be assigned theatre time with both surgeons and you'll be on a one in two call roster for nights. Are you living far from the hospital?'

'I'm in the house-surgeons' quarters,' Anna had replied.

'Good.' For the first time Erica had seemed pleasantly surprised. 'You won't need a room for nights on call, then.'

Anna wasn't so sure it was a good thing. The single bedsitting room was confined and uninspiring. The common room had a rather worn and sad atmosphere and was often deserted. The hospital food in the cafeteria was also uninspiring. If she remained as busy as she was now, however, it wouldn't really matter that much.

Anna had no time to use the common room, no time to really taste the food she bolted when the opportunity arose and was so tired that she usually fell asleep before she had a chance to register how depressing her room was. In any case it was by far the cheapest option for accommodation. Her salary this year was going to have to go in trying to reduce the debt she'd accumulated by her determination to follow a medical training.

'I assume you can find your way around the hospital by now,' Erica summed up.

'I can find the orthopaedic wards, X-Ray, Intensive Care, Theatres and the cafeteria,' Anna responded confidently. Erica was not amused by the final location. Anna sighed inwardly at the cool stare she received. Clearly, it wasn't going to be easy to get on friendly terms with her immediate superior.

'I suggest you get familiar with the rest of the hospital as soon as possible,' Erica stated briskly. 'In particular the paediatric and geriatric wards, although we can have patients in virtually any area. We can't afford to have you wasting time by getting lost.'

Ken was much more encouraging. 'Just tell me or Erica when things are too much to cope with,' he advised. 'We're quite happy to help out with the occasional admission. We don't even mind putting in an IV line or two and we definitely need practice in giving orders over the phone. All part of the training to be a consultant, you know. And don't let Erica scare you. She doesn't live up to her name and she's very good at her job. She passed her Part 1 on her first go,' he added wistfully. 'I hope I do as well.'

That's something I definitely won't have to worry about, Anna reminded herself. After only the short space of a week she knew with absolute certainty that she didn't want a hospital-based career. The pressure was overwhelming, the limited contact with patients was frustrating and her physical exhaustion unbearable. She was on call every second night and so far hadn't made it as far as her own bed. A snatched hour or two of dozing in an armchair didn't set her up well for the incessant round of daytime duties. It was her third night on tonight and she hadn't even been near the armchair.

It was a simple task to increase Mr Ellison's postoperative pain relief. There was no evidence of any complications from the surgery and he was well within the safety margins for the narcotic analgesia he had been charted. Anna was more concerned with the imminent arrival of Molly Smith. The emergency department registrar had obviously been feeling as tired as Anna. The information she'd received over the phone had been to the point.

'She's seventy-four, lives alone, got up during the night, had a dizzy spell and fell over. Came in complaining of pain in her hip and leg, minor contusion to her elbow. Vital signs all OK, her notes are coming up with her. Hip and chest X-rays done. Left hip's badly fractured, no signs of pneumonia or heart failure on X-ray. We've put her in Buck's extension traction to control muscle spasm so she's not in much pain. No sign of a current MI on monitor but she's in chronic A-Fib and hasn't had a 12-lead ECG yet.'

'OK.' Anna had been scribbling in her notebook. 'I'll take care of that.' And that would only be a minor part. Anna's job was to complete the admission formalities and make sure Mrs Smith was ready for surgery first thing in the morning. Taking a history and doing a physical examination on a distressed elderly lady could be a time-consuming and frustrating business.

'It would be another Smith,' she muttered wearily yet again. Anna tried to look on the bright side. Perhaps the more exposure she had the less meaning the name would have and then she could get over her irritating preoccupation with it. Him, she corrected herself. It wasn't as if it was even his real name. Anna could barely repress a shudder at what could have happened if he'd been telling the truth. While Ken had been showing her around the department on her first day he'd mentioned the absent consultant,

Michael Smith, and Anna had almost choked on her coffee.

'He—he doesn't call himself Mike and drive a red Porsche by any chance, does he?' she'd ventured timidly.

Ken's eyebrows had shot up as he'd laughed. 'Are you kidding? He's a BMW man, mean and black, like himself. And he doesn't even get called Michael. It's either Mr Smith or…' Ken glanced around and then lowered his voice to a whisper. 'Jaws!'

'Pardon?'

'His name's Michael George, but Jaws is much more appropriate than George.'

'Why is that?'

'He cruises around waiting for you to slip up and then… *Snap!* Sharks, you know. *Jaws*?' Ken pinched his nostrils together and his voice became a menacing rumble. *'Doo do Doo do Doo do.'*

His imitation of the movie sound effects was so good that Anna laughed delightedly. Then she looked worried. 'He's not really that bad, is he?'

'Let's just say that if straws had been passed around for registrar appointments I'd say that Erica definitely got the short one. What did you mean about a red Porsche?'

'Forget it,' Anna said hurriedly. 'It's not relevant and I'd rather forget it myself.'

'Jaws' was due to return to work in a matter of hours. Molly Smith was to be his patient so, despite her exhaustion and the time of night, Anna wasn't going to skip all but the essential observations. She'd never been shark fodder and was determined not to slip up in any way. Mrs Molly Smith was going to be treated to the de-luxe admission. Luckily her patient was alert, co-operative and in surprisingly little distress after her injury.

The old lady smiled cheerfully at Anna when she arrived at her bedside. 'I'm so sorry to get you out of bed, dear,' she said apologetically. 'What a dreadful time to bother you.'

'It's not a problem, Mrs Smith.' Anna had returned the smile. 'I wasn't in bed.'

'Call me Molly, dear. Goodness, but you look far too young to be a doctor.'

'I'm Dr Kessel. Anna,' she added. 'And I'm only just a doctor but don't worry—I won't be doing your operation. I'm just here to check you out and make sure we have all the information we need. Can you tell me what happened?'

'I got out of bed!' Molly sounded surprised. 'I don't usually and I can't really remember why I did. Then I got a little dizzy and the next thing I knew I could hear Blossom barking. Did I tell you about Blossom?'

'No.' Anna was making notes. She would have to try and determine what had led to the dizzy spell and possible loss of consciousness. Her heart condition was likely to be associated with high blood pressure. The possibility of a silent heart attack had been looked at but a stroke was another consideration.

'Blossom saved my life. She's a darling.' Molly beamed at Anna. 'Do you have any pets, dear?'

'No.' Anna was still writing. She didn't have time to look after herself let alone any animals.

'Blossom's a chihuahua. She's only little but she makes a lot of noise. She woke up my neighbour, Elaine. Goodness knows how long I would have been lying on the floor otherwise. I could have starved to death!'

'Was that the first dizzy spell you've had?'

'Oh, no, dear! I get them quite often. Especially when I get out of bed. It's been worse in the last few days, I think.'

Anna reached for a blood pressure cuff. It was quite possible that a drop in blood pressure on standing could account for both dizzy spells and a fall but, being unable to stand her patient up, it would be difficult to ascertain.

'Are you on any treatment for your blood pressure?'

'I take lots of pills, dear.'

Anna tried to stifle a wave of exhaustion as she unwrapped the cuff again. One-fifty over ninety lying down—no problem there. She wished her patient could be a little more specific. It felt like this was going to be a very long process.

'Can you remember what they are?'

'Well, there's some little white ones. Water pills, I think the doctor called them.'

Anna nodded. A diuretic was a likely treatment for hypertension.

'Then there's the little blue ones. I take two of them every night.'

Anna smiled with satisfaction. She knew what those were. Digoxin for controlling the arrhythmia. She would have to test for digoxin toxicity. It could be another explanation for the old lady's fall. The fact that she'd thought of that possibility should impress Jaws. Anna scribbled rapidly.

'Then there's the rat poison.' Molly Smith chirruped with laughter. 'I love telling people I take rat poison!'

'Is that warfarin?'

'That's right, dear.'

Anna made another note. An indication of the anticoagulant blood levels were a must before surgery. She felt pleased she could remember the form she'd need, without having to look it up, having done one only the day before. INR it was called—an International Normalised Ratio. She would have to type and crossmatch four to six units of blood as well. Molly would be losing some blood from the fracture and would lose more from the surgery.

Anna began her physical examination, looking for pulses in both hips and feet, checking other joints for deformity and eliciting information about previous fractures, surgery or arthritis. When she paused to make notes Molly tried to keep her entertained by telling her about Blossom's many escapades. Apparently Blossom could catch mice, choose her own meals from the refrigerator or pantry and had bitten the daily help on three occasions.

'She won't eat dog food,' Molly confided. 'Blossom thinks she's a person.'

'Who's looking after Blossom for you?' Anna queried.

'My neighbour, Elaine, said she would.' Molly frowned. 'I do hope she's kind to her. Blossom bit Elaine last week, you know.'

'I'm sure she will.' Anna tried to sound confident. She moved on with her examination to try and rule out a stroke. It was now nearly 5 a.m. but Anna was going to be thorough. She looked at her patient's pupil size and range of eye and facial movements.

Checking lip movement, Anna asked Molly to show her her teeth.

'But they're not my teeth, dear!'

Anna smiled a little wearily. 'Show me anyway.'

She got Molly to hold up her arms, shrug her shoulders and resist hand pressure as she checked the power in her patient's limbs. Anna looked at her skin and jugular venous pressure to try and assess any volume depletion, which would be another important consideration for surgery. She took a 12-lead ECG and drew blood for tests. Finally, at 5.45 a.m., Anna excused herself, having explained the procedure of a hip replacement to Molly's satisfaction. She settled at the nurses' station to write up her copious notes and fill in all the requisition forms for the bloods.

Determined to impress 'Jaws' when he cruised in for the morning round, Anna summarised the notes into a personal shorthand she'd developed at medical school and copied them into the notebook she carried with her at all times. It was then that her fatigue really kicked in and she had to concentrate on ticking the correct boxes on the blood-test requisition forms while the longing for a strong cup of coffee became relentless. There was no INR form available on the desk. Anna began to search through drawers, looking for a fresh supply.

The sound of the cardiac-arrest alarm on her pager shocked the exhaustion into retreat and Anna ran to a nearby ward, fighting the fear that she might not be able to handle the emergency until a crash team arrived. She'd studied and regurgitated resuscitation procedures endlessly, and had practised CPR repeatedly on the class dummy they'd named Beavis until she'd felt far too intimately acquainted with the life-like replica. She'd even observed an arrest as a sixth-year student. Perhaps it was one of those things when she just had to take the plunge and get on with it.

As it happened, she wasn't required to apply any theoretical skills. The young nurse had been too late in raising the alarm and the elderly patient had clearly died some time previously. Anna, having been prepared to launch herself into a life-preserving battle, felt deflated and a little confused. Unsure of what was required, she awaited the arrival of the crash team and observed the techniques for documenting the incident. She even waited for the arrival of the enclosed and draped stretcher which would transfer the patient to the morgue.

It was all part of a learning experience, but at 6.30 a.m. after a sleepless night Anna found it all a bit much. The longed-for cup of coffee sat cooling on a table before her as Anna buried her face in her folded arms.

It was the insistent beeping of her pager that woke her. A sudden thought that it was another cardiac-arrest alarm caused Anna to jerk to her feet, but a check of the telephone number displayed showed that it was the orthopaedic ward, trying to contact her. Another glance at her watch told Anna it was 7.45 a.m. She'd been asleep for an hour in her chair in the small relatives' room she had escaped to. A splash of cold water on her face and a quick hair comb and she could be back on the ward in five minutes. As she reached for the wall phone, however, the door beside it burst open and Ken appeared.

'There you are, Anna! Quick, "Jaws" is on the warpath.'

'I've got a beep to answer.'

'That's Erica, trying to find you. The ward round started fifteen minutes ago. He's not impressed. In fact, I've never seen him so grumpy.'

'Fifteen minutes ago,' Anna echoed. 'That was 7.30 a.m. Who the hell starts a ward round at 7.30 a.m.?'

'Sharky Smith, that's who. He does it simply to keep his junior staff on their toes. Start dancing, Anna, or you'll sink before you even get a chance to swim.' Ken pinched his nostrils. *'Doo do—'*

'Not funny, Ken.' Anna cut him off. She felt nervous enough already. Arriving on the ward at a run, Anna slowed as she passed the nurses' station—stopping only long enough to grab Molly Smith's results from the in-basket. She was frantically scanning them as she hurried towards the patient's room. She couldn't see Erica, the consultant or any of the senior nursing staff. Anna unhooked Molly's chart from the end of her bed to check her most recent observations.

'How are you, Molly?'

'I'm worried, dear. Very worried.' Mrs Smith looked much less cheerful this morning.

'About the surgery?' Anna rested her fingers on her patient's pulse.

'Oh, no, dear. It's Blossom. I'm sure Elaine won't remember that she has to have a scrambled egg for her breakfast. With a little piece of chopped-up toast.'

Anna swallowed. 'I'm sure Blossom will be just fine. Try not to worry, Molly.'

'But—' Mrs Smith's wavering response was curtailed as her curtains were whisked aside. Anna was still smiling reassuringly at her patient. The sarcastic inflection of the male voice cut through her senses like a knife.

'Dr Van Kessel. How kind of you to join us.'

Frightened, Anna's wide gaze flew up and across the bed. She found herself staring at the face of the man she'd spent the last ten days trying desperately to forget. She felt a faint wave of nausea and gripped the side of the bed for support. *Mike!* His name was trying to force itself from her numb lips. 'M-Mr Smith,' she managed to stammer, and then added rather inanely, 'How do you do?'

'I'm more interested in how our patient is doing, Dr Van Kessel.' He emphasised the 'Van' but Anna had to hand it to him. He didn't miss a beat. Nobody could have any idea they had ever met before, let alone—

'I'm a bit worried, Doctor,' Molly told her consultant. 'About Blossom.'

Michael Smith looked at Molly with incredulity. It was almost as though he was surprised to find a patient who could speak, Anna thought. Molly blinked in confusion.

Erica sighed very lightly. 'Perhaps you'd like to present this patient, Anna. You have admitted her, I take it?'

'Of course.' Anna whipped out her notebook. She began to recite Mrs Smith's past medical history and findings on examination but was interrupted by the consultant.

'It might be very commendable to document the removal of a plantar wart ten years ago, Doctor, but it has little relevance to the present situation.'

'Mrs Smith suffered complications from the removal of the wart. She got an infection that required hospital admission and—'

'What's her blood count?'

Anna turned to the sheaf of result forms in her hand and read out the required levels.

'Digoxin level?'

'Two point six five. It's a bit high,' Anna added helpfully. 'I thought it might explain the dizzy spells in the absence of any neurological findings.'

'Thank you for that.' Michael Smith's tone didn't imply any form of gratitude. 'What's the INR?'

Anna ruffled the forms again. Molly sighed loudly in the ensuing silence and the staff all glanced in her direction whereupon she burst into tears.

'It's Blossom,' she sobbed. 'I know Elaine won't be looking after her properly.'

Michael Smith looked disgusted. He glared at Anna as though she were responsible for upsetting the patient.

'What's this about?' he snapped.

'Blossom,' Anna explained hurriedly. 'She bit Elaine last week and—'

'For God's sake.' Michael Smith stepped aside. He held out his hand commandingly. 'Give me those results.'

Anna waited as the consultant flicked through them. Out of the corner of her eye she could see the nursing staff comforting Molly. Erica had a long-suffering expression on her face. Incompetence from juniors was, after all, only to be expected. Anna felt a cold shiver up her spine as she realised why the queried result was not available.

'Why is the INR not here?' The query was another snap.

'There were no forms available,' Anna confessed wearily. 'I got called to an—'

'I'm not remotely interested in your excuses. Do

you have any idea how critical it is to know the degree of anticoagulation, before subjecting someone to surgery?'

'Yes. Sir,' Anna couldn't help adding. She straightened her back. She wasn't going to let him rip her into little pieces without a struggle. 'It was an unfortunate—'

The interruption was instant and curt. 'It certainly was. Do you know how long it takes for vitamin K to stop or reverse the effects of warfarin if that's required before surgery?'

'Some hours, I believe.' Anna took a deep breath. 'But the effect of fresh frozen plasma is almost immediate.'

The look she received made Anna feel as if she'd just crawled out from under a rock. She knew that Erica and the nursing staff were watching and listening.

'It's common medical practice these days to avoid giving blood products unless the situation is urgent. Treatment for a fracture such as Mrs Smith's is considered urgent but there's another reason why that option is contraindicated. Given Mrs Smith's age and cardiac history, I might even expect you to be aware of that, Doctor.'

Anna remained silent.

'Well?' The prompt was icy.

'The potential for putting the patient into heart failure,' Anna replied quietly. The knowledge was there. It was the strain of trying to extract all the relevant pieces and apply them under pressure that made things so difficult. This situation would have been humiliating had Michael Smith been the complete stranger Anna had expected. As it was, it was virtually unbearable. She was grateful when he turned away.

'See that an INR is done immediately and then get the result to me. In person,' he added forcefully. He turned to his registrar. 'We're going to have to delay Mrs Smith's surgery until early this afternoon at least. Get onto Theatre, Erica, and do some juggling.' He stepped nearer his patient. 'I do apologise for this, Mrs Smith. I realise how upsetting it must be for you.'

'I'm just upset about Blossom, dear,' Molly told him earnestly. 'Did you know that she bit Elaine last week?'

'I'm sure Dr Van Kessel will help you sort it out,' the consultant said smoothly. 'It's what she's here for.'

Anna took the blood sample from Molly and despatched it for urgent measurement. She filed the results she had and even rang Elaine to enquire after Blossom's well-being. She didn't relay Molly's neighbour's caustic opinion of dogs that resembled rats but was able to tell her honestly that Blossom was being well looked after and had had a chocolate biscuit for breakfast.

'Oh, the naughty girl!'

Anna was unsure whether it was Blossom or Elaine being referred to but didn't enquire. She had three patients asking to see her. Mr Smith and Erica had gone to Theatre. Their full ward round wasn't scheduled until tomorrow morning. They'd only come to review that morning's theatre cases. Mr McPherson's round was, however, due to get under way and Anna was too busy for some time to even think about what was going to happen when the INR result appeared. When it did arrive, mid-morning, Anna was re-

lieved to find it within normal range. Mrs Smith
would be able to go up to Theatre immediately. She
expressed her relief to the senior nurse nearby but
Sally shook her head.

'No, she won't be able to go.'

'Why not? This result's fine.'

'Yes, but she's just had a cup of tea.'

'Oh, no.'

'You'd better take that result through to Mr Smith.
He's probably finished the case they had first thing.'

'Where will I find him?'

'Try his office.' Sally pointed vaguely down the
corridor. 'Otherwise you could go up to Theatre or
beep him.'

Beeping the consultant and giving the information
by phone was an attractive option but Anna knew it
wouldn't be acceptable. At some point they were going to have to meet privately and some mention was
going to have to be made of their previous encounter.
She may as well bite the bullet and get it over with.

CHAPTER TWO

THE office door was firmly and uninvitingly closed.

Anna paused for a long moment, before knocking. The name plate was discreet, simply, M.G. SMITH. Anna heard an echo of her own voice. 'Pull the other one, Mike—it's got bells on it!' Maybe one day it might seem funny but right now amusement was the last emotional response Anna was capable of summoning.

The office area was on the same floor as the orthopaedic wards but in a separate wing that was well away from the general hospital bustle. It seemed quite peaceful. The large office housing the three departmental secretaries was also quiet, emitting only the muted sound of keyboard tapping. The women were intent on their screens, cut off from communication by the earphones that allowed them to replay the dictation they had accumulated. They couldn't see Anna and she shut her eyes for a second to gather her strength. The sound of the keyboards faded and Anna had a sudden memory of what a genuinely peaceful place was like.

A calm stretch of river visible between the trunks of the numerous trees bordering its banks. The intense heat of the sun dissipated by the greenery, the light dappled with stars of sunshine glinting as the leaves moved in the soft breeze. Clear calls of bellbirds high in the canopy but the enchantment of fantails at much closer quarters.

It had been the epitome of what she'd been searching for on her hard-earned and first ever holiday, and
Anna could almost forget the frustration of trying to
erect a tent for the first time. She could forget the
weariness of the long walk into the camping ground
from the main road, the blisters the new boots had
given her and the backache from the unfamiliar pack
she'd carried. Anna had removed the heavy boots and
had stood, basking in the beauty and serenity of her
surroundings, clad only in her denim cut-offs and
light singlet top. Within a short time she'd felt re-
freshed and ready to tackle her difficult task with re-
newed determination.

Even the memory of those few minutes was enough
to inspire Anna. Her eyes flickered open but her feet
refused to obey the command to step nearer to the
forbidding door. In fact, they took a step backwards.
Anna swore softly under her breath then caught herself. It had been her unladylike habit of swearing
which had helped get her into this mess in the first
place.

Anna paced a few steps down the corridor and
back, not yet ready to face M.G. Smith. An office
door opposite her stood open. It belonged to the head
of department, Tim McPherson, and was unoccupied
at present. A third office was shared by the registrars,
Erica and Ken. House surgeons didn't even merit office space. They perched where they could, usually
fighting for a peaceful spot on busy nursing stations
to do battle with seemingly endless deluges of paperwork.

This office area was for those who'd survived the
trial by fire Anna had entered. Those on the way up
and those who'd arrived and were now in the position

to control Anna's environment. She knew it was within their power to make or break her in her chosen profession and she didn't feel confident that she was going to survive this new obstacle.

Perhaps her initial impression of Michael Smith had, in fact, been correct—that he was arrogant, judgemental, prejudiced and over-privileged. She should just forget what had happened later and remember simply how they'd met—or, better yet, how they'd parted. She'd gone over it dozens of times already, amazed that her initial reaction had been erased so completely by what had come afterwards. Even the ending hadn't been enough to negate the overall effect. Maybe it would help her now if she could summon up the anger again.

Of course, it had been a series of small things which had contributed to her ill-temper at the time. The heat of the day, the unpleasant camp manager and especially the uncooperative tent. Even arming herself with a tent pole like a spear and going into battle hadn't gained her any ground. How had the stupid tent managed to fold itself around her like that? And how could she have missed the sound of a vehicle approaching? Surely she hadn't been cursing quite that loudly.

It had been the laughter which had alerted Anna to her audience and had also caused her temper to soar to new heights as she'd finally managed to disentangle herself from the canvas shroud. Still holding her pole, she'd glared around her, narrowing her eyes against the still harsh light. It must have been the camp manager, checking up on her, and it had been the perfect time to tell him exactly where to get off.

Bearing an unfortunate resemblance to her father,

the aging, overweight man had almost drooled when she'd checked in, seemingly convinced that her voice had been emanating from either her legs or her chest.

'The camp's pretty deserted right now,' he informed Anna's legs, 'what with the school holidays being over, but you'll be quite safe, love. I'm always here. You can't see my hut from your camp site but I'm within easy screaming distance.' The smile was more of a leer. 'Scream anytime,' he suggested on leaving.

But the deep tones Anna heard now were nothing like the manager's.

'I suppose you'd like some help.'

Anna's gaze fastened on the speaker and her eyes narrowed further. The amused tone of the query had been heavily overlaid with insinuation. A hint of resigned willingness to help out yet another damsel in distress. The confident masculinity emanating from the tall figure before her suggested that he had plenty of experience in dealing with damsels—in distress or otherwise.

'No, I wouldn't, actually,' Anna snapped. 'Why should you suppose that?'

'I haven't heard language like that since I walked past the changing rooms of our high-school rugby team. They'd just lost an important match.'

Anna was still glaring at the man as he spoke. Walking past the changing room would be right, she thought. Playing rugby was not nearly sophisticated enough to interest this man as a pastime and his build was too slender, despite the width of shoulder. Her gaze flicked down the length of his body and then behind him. The red, open-topped Porsche looked brand-new, gleaming elegantly under the shade of her tree. *Her* tree! The tent pole in her hand jerked involuntarily. Her tone was dismissive.

'I don't require your assistance so don't let me hold you up. You can get a much better view of the river from down there.' Anna pointed with the pole.

'I'm sure you can. But this happens to be my camp site.'

'No, it's my camp site. As you can see, I'm putting up my tent. Here. On this site.'

The man laughed again, acknowledging the failure of her efforts. He pointed to the stick in the ground near her tangled pile of canvas.

'You're site number 16—is that right?'

'Yes.' Anna was seething. She might be having difficulty erecting her tent but it didn't give him the right to assume such an arrogant air of superiority.

'And I'm site number 17. Right here, see?' He spoke deliberately, as though she might have difficulty understanding.

'That's ridiculous. They're far too close together.'

'People don't need much space to put up a tent.' He hesitated as his lips quirked. 'Usually. Besides, it's a popular camping ground.'

'Not at the moment. Up until five minutes ago I was the only person here. Go and see the manager. I'm sure he can find you somewhere else.'

'Perhaps his choice was deliberate.' The man frowned. 'You're not here on your own, are you?'

'That's none of your business.'

'You must be mad.'

'Oh?' The anger in Anna's tone was obvious. 'Why is that?'

'A girl like you, on her own, in an isolated spot like this?'

'What exactly is a girl like me?' Anna's ponytail had almost fallen out during her struggle with the tent. She flicked back some strands of long blonde hair and waited with an inward groan. This man wouldn't drool, of course, but the appreciation and invitation would be there. It always was. Anna was used to men's reaction to her physical appearance—was sick to death of it, in fact. They saw only her body, never bothered to consider it might house a brain as well. To her surprise the man merely shook his head slightly and turned back to his car.

'Have it your own way,' he said pleasantly. 'I came here for some peace and quiet, not an argument.'

'You might get more peace if you camp somewhere else,' Anna retorted. 'Go and find site number 2 or 102.'

'I've paid for site number 17. Camp regulations are to camp on your assigned site. I like this site. It has a very nice tree. Besides, I don't break regulations.'

'I'm sure you don't.' Anna eyed his back with resentment. The shorts and T-shirt he was wearing looked appropriate but not quite right somehow, as though he was unused to wearing them. He was too groomed—like his car. She watched him lifting bulky objects from the back of the car. Everything about him shouted wealth, an easy road through life, getting exactly what he wanted. Everything that Anna had never had. She turned away in disgust.

'By the way, you'll find the pole fits better on the outside of the tent.'

Anna ignored him but cringed inwardly. Of course! That had been why she couldn't find the hole when she'd been crawling around inside. She began to straighten the tent's edges, studiously avoiding any sideways glances. Becoming confident that she could not complete her task, Anna was irritated by the commanding tone behind her.

'Move that peg further out. You won't have enough tension on the rope that close.'

Anna's hand tightened around the smooth rock she was using to hammer in the pegs. She turned her head slowly. 'You like giving orders, don't you?'

'I was merely giving you some advice. Feel free to ignore it if you don't mind your tent collapsing on you in the middle of the night.' His tone was cool as he turned away abruptly. Not only did he like giving orders, he was clearly accustomed to having them obeyed.

Anna did move the peg but her annoyance made her glance in his direction, vainly hoping to find fault with her neighbour's efforts. Of course, his tent was already erected, the tension on his guy ropes admirably strong.

'I'll bet you usually wear a suit,' Anna found herself saying.

He looked up, surprised. Anna noticed the unusual colour of his hazel eyes. They had a golden tint to them that made her think of a lion. As the look of surprise gave way to one of annoyance, the gaze of the tawny eyes fastened on her with an appropriately predatory glare. Anna suddenly felt nervous. Reaching for another tent peg, she wished she'd kept her thought to herself.

'What's that supposed to mean?' The rich drawl was deceptively pleasant.

'Not much.' Anna verbally scrambled for cover but then she missed the tent peg with her stone and hit her finger. She cursed roundly.

'For God's sake, use a hammer!' An object was dropped to the ground beside her. 'How can you possibly expect to do a job properly if you don't use the correct tools.'

Anna took her fingertip out of her mouth as she jumped to her feet. 'You think I'm some sort of idiot, don't you?'

'I'm sure there are some things you're probably quite good at.' The leonine eyes took a lazy route down the length of her body. Anna was suddenly intensely aware of just how short her cut-offs were and the fact that she wasn't wearing a bra beneath the soft cotton singlet. At least his eyes managed to return to her face. She took a deep breath.

'I think you're possibly the most arrogant person I've ever met,' she informed him. 'You invade my privacy, ridicule what I'm doing and order me around like I'm some sort of minion in your office. Just because you're rich enough to have a dinky little hammer for your precious tent pegs doesn't give you an automatic superiority over me.' Anna realised she was enjoying giving vent to her accumulated grievances. 'Now you've got some preconceived notion of what I do for a living and you not only assume you're correct, you assume that it can't possibly be anything that requires even a minimal amount of intelligence. Just what do you think I am? A masseuse?'

An eyebrow lifted sardonically. 'Are you?'

Anna gave a silent whistle. 'You are unbelievable,' she snarled.

'You're more articulate that I might have expected,' her adversary commented, 'but I'm not the only one making assumptions here. You assume I usually wear a suit. What is it that you think I am?'

'Probably a lawyer,' Anna snapped. 'I'm sure you'd thoroughly enjoy ripping people to shreds on a witness stand. You could be a financier or you could be a brain surgeon. I can just see you hurling instruments around an operating theatre and shouting at people. But I expect you're a C.E.O of some large business—with an over-inflated pay packet and an ego to match.' Anna paused for breath. 'Why don't you go and hire a yacht and find some more suitable company?'

'I might just do that.' The man began to walk towards his car. 'And why don't you give up trying to do things you're not competent at and find a man to look after you?' He opened the door of his car and slid easily behind the wheel. 'A very tolerant man,' he added.

Anna watched him leave, astonished. Surely he wasn't simply going to disappear and leave his camping equipment behind? Then she shrugged. Clearly the dislike was mutual and he could probably afford half a dozen tents without blinking. He'd probably gone off to buy a yacht. Anna eyed her own second-hand and rather patched shelter with a sigh. Then she smiled. At least it was up now. She could relax and enjoy herself, which had, after all, been the object of the exercise.

Annoyingly, the tension wouldn't go away. Anna unpacked and sorted through the rest of her pack but her gaze kept straying to the neatly zipped, bright, new tent nearby. The image of its owner refused to go away as well and Anna found herself remembering details she hadn't realised she'd noticed. The day's growth of beard on a determined looking jaw, the dark eyelashes and brows that matched the recently cut wavy hair that framed them. The expensive-looking watch but no rings on either hand. His voice had been very deep and he sounded well educated. Well, he would be, wouldn't he? It went with the arrogance.

Anna had come across plenty of similar people. Her class at medical school had had more than a few. They'd had all the advantages—comfortable places to live, able to afford the latest textbooks, ample time to study and the ultimate luxury of time to socialise and have fun.

Anna had never joined them. Finding time to study—that had been her luxury. Lonely hours squeezed in between lectures and the vital, never-ending part-time employment that had allowed her to survive financially. Well, almost survive. The alarming size of the debt she now had with the bank had been mitigated only by her sense of triumph at her recent graduation. Not only graduation but at the top of her class! The debt, the struggle, the loneliness—even her parents' disapproval—had all seemed worth it.

Anna had broken free. Her personal celebration was a week of holiday—the first in her life. Even now she had tried to make it constructive. Due to take up her first house-surgeon position in the North Island township of Tauranga, Anna was using the week to explore the surrounding countryside, moving north up the Coromandel Peninsula, after exploring Tauranga for two days.

Unsure whether to visit the small settlement of Tairua or Pauanui first, Anna had asked the bus driver to let her off on the main road at the turn-off. Seeing the signpost to Broken Hills, Anna had consulted her guidebook and followed her instincts. The place had sounded magical. She'd camp for a night and explore the old gold-workings tomorrow.

The light was softening but the heat of the day was still intense even at 7 p.m. Deciding it was time for a swim, Anna changed into her bathing suit. She was dismayed to find it much tighter than she remembered but, then, she'd hardly worn it for years. Her figure had matured considerably since her late teens and the thin fabric of the suit was now stretched uncomfortably across her breasts. Anna pulled on a T-shirt as well.

Stooping for her towel, her gaze was caught by a large and unusual possession. She'd told herself she was mad, strapping her guitar to the back of her pack, but the thought of being able to indulge in an almost forgotten passion had been irresistible. Anna picked up the instrument lovingly. The swim could wait a while longer. The effects of her earlier confrontation had receded and her surroundings felt peaceful again. Almost too peaceful. Music could be the perfect antidote.

Settled cross-legged under the tree, Anna tuned her guitar carefully, strummed a few chords then began to sing quietly. Music and sports had been her escape as she'd grown up, the only acceptable form of independence within the rigid confines of family and community discipline. Medical school and part-time work had consigned both leisure activities almost to a dim memory, but the sense of freedom and individuality they could bestow began to return to Anna as the rusty feeling melted from her fingers. She stopped singing and began instead to play a classical piece, the harmony a joy as her swift plucking regained its old skill.

She saw, rather than heard, the return of the sports car but didn't miss a note. For some reason the pleasure in both her activity and her surroundings went up a notch or two and she bent her head, sheltering her face with a silky curtain of hair as she allowed herself to become lost in the emotion of the music she was creating. It wasn't until the piece was completed that she became aware of how much her fingers hurt. The protection of callouses had long gone and the steel strings had left painful grooves. She laid the guitar down reluctantly.

'That was very impressive.'

Anna glanced up. The man looked familiar now and she was amazed that she felt so pleased at his return. She dismissed the feeling.

'Thank you,' she answered coolly. 'It just happens to be one of the things I'm "quite good at".' The pleasure she felt in throwing his phrase back at him with a somewhat sarcastic inflection wasn't lost on Anna. The man might be insufferable but his company certainly couldn't be considered boring.

He wasn't going to bite this time, however. He held his hands up, palms outward, in a gesture of surrender. 'Look—' His hands dropped. 'What's your name, anyway?'

'Anna. Anna Kessel. What's yours?'

'Mike.' The response was brusque. Anna had the impression that personal information was not imparted willingly. A surname was not forthcoming. 'Look, Anna. We're both here on holiday, presumably to enjoy ourselves. We're both adults and for better

or worse we're going to be neighbours for the night.
I'm sure we're both capable of being civil about it.'

'Is that one of the camp regulations?' Anna found
herself smiling at him for the first time.

'If it isn't, it should be. Now…' Mike gestured
towards his car '…I just went into Pauanui for something to eat and I've got some fish and chips which
should at least be warm. Would you like to share
them?'

Anna hesitated. The invitation was decidedly unexpected. In her view a civil relationship with this
man would probably mean keeping as much distance
as possible between them at all times.

His tone became more inviting. 'It's fresh snap-
per—caught locally today. And I've got a cold bottle
of Chardonnay to go with it.'

'OK.' Anna scrambled to her feet. It was nearly
eight and she suddenly realised how incredibly hun-
gry she was. As she caught the aroma of the package
Mike was opening the bread and cheese in her pack
lost any appeal they might have had. 'Thanks,' she
added belatedly. At least he'd invited rather than ordered her to eat with him.

Sitting under the tree, they ate the food straight
from the wrappers and drank the wine from plastic
tumblers. Anna thought it was the most delicious
meal she'd ever eaten and enthusiastically accepted
the last portion of the fish.

'Haven't you eaten for a while?' Mike enquired.

'Not today,' Anna admitted. 'It was too hot.'

He shook his head disapprovingly and Anna felt a
stirring of irritation. 'I was going to,' she stated de-
fensively. 'Despite your impression of me, I'm quite
capable of taking care of myself.' She picked up her

tumbler then paused. 'Is that why you brought the food back? To save me from blowing myself up, trying to ignite a Primus?'

He still wasn't biting. 'What made you come to Broken Hills?' he asked calmly.

'It sounded interesting. I'm going to walk up and look at the gold-workings tomorrow.'

'That's quite a stiff climb. There are some quite long ladders up rock faces.'

'I expect I'll manage.' Anna's tone was cool. She flicked him a quick glance. 'And if I can't, I'm sure some man will pop out of the woodwork and offer to rescue me.'

His glance was speculative. 'I suppose you're actually a professional alpine guide when you're not on holiday.'

'In between stints at the massage parlour?' Anna grinned.

'What is it with you and massage parlours?' Mike frowned. 'Is that really where you work?'

'No, it isn't.' Anna drained the last of her wine. 'I suppose it's my reaction to the attitudes I've come across rather too much. I don't like people being labelled. It's too easy to box everything according to black and white expectations or opinions. People who do it are either lazy or intolerant.'

'I don't quite see the connection.'

Anna sighed. 'If you're blonde it has to come out of a bottle. If you're presentably good-looking as well as blonde then you probably don't have a brain. If you've got a halfway decent body then you're bound to be involved in the sex industry in some form.' She narrowed her eyes at her companion. 'If you're female and on your own then you must be hunting for a man.'

'And you're not, obviously.'

'Not what? Hunting for a man, involved with the sex industry, a natural blonde or presentably good-looking?'

'I can answer the last one myself—in the affirmative.'

Anna snorted ungraciously. 'I don't bleach my hair. I'm definitely not hunting for a man and I have no interest in the sex industry. Satisfied?'

'No. What *do* you do?'

'I'm a...' Anna hesitated and glanced at Mike. She sensed that his interest was caught but for some reason she was reluctant to tell him her hard-won title of doctor. It was too precious an achievement to risk having it disbelieved or belittled in some way. She cleared her throat. 'I just finished a waitressing job last week,' she told him quite truthfully. 'I'm having a few days' break before I start something new.'

'Ah.' There was a short silence. Then it was Mike's turn to clear his throat. 'Your attempt to box me in a suit as an unfeeling lawyer, temperamental surgeon or dictatorial manager was simply to point out the error of my own ways, I take it?'

'Absolutely.' Anna beamed at her companion. 'Was it effective?'

'Temporarily, at least.' Mike returned her grin and Anna was startled at the way his face changed and softened. Confused, she dropped her gaze. 'Let's make the most of it,' he continued. 'Let's forget first impressions and intolerant opinions and enjoy what's left of the evening. Fancy a swim?'

'It's almost dark,' Anna pointed out. 'I don't know the river at all.'

'I do, and it's perfectly safe,' Mike assured her. He rose effortlessly to his feet and stripped off his T-shirt. 'Come on.'

Anna's eyes widened at his sudden near nakedness. She scrambled to her feet then hesitated, her heart thudding. What on earth did she think she was doing? Alone, in an isolated place with a total stranger who was displaying rather a large amount of a powerfully male body. She didn't even like him and if he turned out to be a rapist or murderer she doubted whether the camp manager would be of the slightest assistance no matter how loudly she screamed.

Anna's feet seemed to move forward of their own accord. Instinctively she knew she was standing at an important crossroad in her life. She'd already met the biggest challenge she'd ever set herself in breaking free from her background and proving herself capable of achieving a professional career. She'd never allowed herself to be distracted by a real emotional or physical relationship with anyone. Maybe it was time for a new challenge.

Mike was ahead of her as they reached the river. He walked straight in until the water lapped his thighs and then dived without hesitation. Anna gasped as the water bit her feet. Surely there had to be snow on the ranges somewhere for the water to be this icy. She wasn't about to let Mike see her hesitate, however. Gritting her teeth, she marched in and tried not to think about the dive she was about to make. Discomfort and trepidation were things she'd long since learned to disguise. The aftermath of confrontations with her father had seen to that. She surfaced with another gasp.

'Kind of takes your breath away, doesn't it?' Mike's head was right beside hers. Anna trod water as she nodded. 'You're not scared of eels, are you?'

'Of course not!' Anna tried to sound scornful but she hated the very thought of eels and couldn't help a quick glance over her shoulder. Anything could be lurking in the black depths of this waterhole.

'Are there really eels?' She turned back as she spoke but Mike had vanished. Anna blinked in confusion then shrieked as she felt a nip on her thigh. Mike's head surfaced. He was grinning broadly.

'Got you!'

'You—you *pig*!' Anna shouted. She raised her arm in an instinctive urge to slap him but Mike caught her wrist. Anna's momentum was transferred to her body and she floated closer. Their bodies touched and brushed against each other and Anna gasped yet again as she felt a shock even greater than the embrace the arctic water had given her. There was a moment of shocked silence as their eyes met, the ripples of the pool dying around them.

When their lips met it seemed the only possible progression of events. Anna felt the chill of his lips and then the incredible warmth of his mouth and tongue. Their legs tangled together as they trod water, their bodies brushed and then slid apart. Anna felt the straps of her overtight bathing suit being eased off her shoulders and the water caressed her breasts as if in preparation for the gentle hand that followed. Both naked and still out of their depth, the water made their play astonishingly sensual. It was exhilarating, exciting but increasingly frustrating.

When Mike pulled her closer to the edge of the waterhole and they found their feet on a firm surface Anna followed willingly. The water still provided a cover, the chill of it only adding to the intense heat Anna could feel emanating from Mike's body. She craved the heat—the touch—and cried out in ecstasy as it finally reached within her and the unbearable tension was over in waves of pure warmth. Even when the cold began to make her teeth chatter she didn't want to break the contact. Neither, it appeared, did Mike.

Holding hands and silent, they ran back to the campsite, towelled each other dry and then simply began again, this time in the cocoon of Anna's tiny tent. The flap was left open, the calls of the moreporks and the startling brightness of the stars only adding to the background of an experience Anna couldn't believe.

There seemed no need to talk. Words would only have detracted from the communication of their bodies, and it was a conversation that felt as if it could never be complete. Questions were asked and answered, anxieties soothed, promises given and received. The stars had faded into the first light of dawn before sleep claimed Anna, but she hadn't noticed. Her only awareness was of the warmth of this man beside her, of the incredible gift he'd given her in awakening her body and the joyful anticipation of continuation.

It was the heat that woke her. Trickles of perspiration down her legs and back. The flap on the tent was closed and the air was suffocating. Pulling open the flap, Anna looked towards site number 17. And then looked again. The site was clear. No tent, no Porsche, not even an empty wine bottle to be seen.

Anna stared, bewildered. Mike had gone, without a word. Simply vanished. Had he, in fact, been there at all? The whole episode had had a dreamlike quality anyway. Something that good could only be dreamt of. But she could still see the indentation of his body on her opened-out sleeping bag, could feel it on her skin. She could still smell and taste him. It had been reality even if now it seemed only fantasy.

Anna finally stopped her pacing. Reality was what was facing her now. It might be difficult to reconcile the memory of such a passionate lover to the grim personality now awaiting her in his office, but hadn't he already proved it had been nothing very special as far as he was concerned? That she'd just been a convenience—just one of the varied ingredients that made up an enjoyable holiday?

Yes. Anna had to admit that he'd proved it only too well. If his mysterious disappearance had been the end of the encounter then the memory could have been enshrined as a magical occurrence. But it hadn't been the end, unfortunately. And what had come later had spoiled everything. The mixed emotions her memories had created distilled into a feeling of humiliation—and anger. OK, so she'd been naïve. But he'd taken advantage of it.

With sudden resolution Anna rapped smartly on the door of M.G. Smith's office.

CHAPTER THREE

'YES!' The bark from within offered no invitation. Clearly, one needed to have very good reason to interrupt Mr Smith.

'What *is* it?'

Anna opened the door. 'I have the INR result on Mrs Smith,' she said without preamble. 'It's 1.2—within normal range.'

Mike made no comment. After what seemed like a long silence he rose from his seat. Crossing the room, he closed the door behind Anna, took the proffered form from her fingers and then returned to his seat, still in silence. Even wearing theatre greens in place of the dark suit he'd had on previously he was no less intimidating. Finally he spoke.

'This is an unexpected situation I find myself in, Dr Van Kessel. Unexpected and, I have to say, most unwelcome.'

Anna said nothing. Her eyes were locked on his. She could see every golden glint in the hazel depths. Her search revealed no hint of warmth, however. How could this man be capable of the extraordinary and gentle passion she'd known with his alter ego?

'When I noted that my first house-surgeon rotation was to be filled by a Dr A. *Van* Kessel, I failed to make any connection that might have enabled an avoidance of this situation. Had you been more honest, this wouldn't have happened.' His gaze flicked down. 'I see your name badge is also inaccurate.'

43

Anna cleared her throat. 'The name on my birth certificate is Annalise Van Kessel. I am obliged to use it on legal documents that require a full name. I have been known as Anna Kessel since I became an adult. My Dutch heritage has no relevance and I prefer to keep things simple.' Anna spoke more firmly. 'I would prefer to be addressed as Dr Kessel. Or Anna.'

'Let me make something simple very clear to you, Dr Van Kessel.' Michael Smith spoke quietly. 'I do not tolerate dishonesty.'

'I didn't lie to you,' Anna defended herself. 'I merely omitted something which should have been totally irrelevant.'

'So that makes it acceptable?' Mike snapped. 'You lied to me about your occupation. You said you were a waitress.'

'No!' Anna felt a flash of temper. 'I told you I'd just finished a waitressing job and was taking a week's break, before starting something new. It was the truth. I had part-time jobs to support myself through medical school. My financial position is such that I had to keep it going as long as possible.' She couldn't help adding, 'If that's any of your business.'

'I'll tell you what *is* my business.' His anger more than matched her own. 'We'll be working together in a professional capacity for the next three months. I will not tolerate any familiarity, discussion of our previous encounter or gossip circulating about myself or my private holiday activities.'

'Familiarity is the last thing I want,' Anna said with conviction. 'And you certainly don't have to be concerned about me revealing any personal information about you. I'd be quite happy to forget we ever met.

Perhaps you'd also prefer to pretend it never happened.'

She saw a flicker in those tawny eyes. Regret? Memory of a night he himself had described as 'perfect'? The impression was gone instantly.

'You're advocating another lie by omission. Do I take it that this is typical behaviour for you, Anna?'

The use of her given name almost undid her. Anna felt suddenly humiliated. She'd stepped out of her 'holiday fling' compartment in this man's life and now she was being punished. She felt like a schoolgirl standing in the headmaster's office and experienced a desperate need to escape.

'I apologise for my error in not obtaining the INR result on Mrs Smith.' Anna couldn't take any more of this personal attack right now. 'She's now scheduled for Theatre at 1 p.m. Will that be all?' She forced herself to meet his eyes again. Did he have any idea how close he was to breaking her? Would he allow her the dignity of retreat?

'Please make yourself available. I will expect to see you in Theatre at precisely 1 p.m.' Michael Smith rose smoothly once again and crossed the room to open the door. 'I don't suffer fools easily, Dr Van Kessel,' he said softly as she passed him. 'I hope you are more competent than first impressions indicate.'

It could have been debated whether Michael Smith slammed the door behind Anna Kessel or whether the closure was merely on the firm side. Had there been anyone to witness it, what would have excited much more comment would have been the ensuing behaviour of Michael Smith, following the firm closure of the office door. Putting his face in his hands, he leaned back against the door. Then his hands dropped to form fists at his sides and his head tilted back to rest on the solid wood, an agonised expression on his face.

It just couldn't be worse! Mike had spent the second week of his holiday attempting—unsuccessfully—to escape a preoccupation with Anna Kessel. The memory of their night together and their acrimonious final parting had tortured him. He'd thought that a return to a hectic work schedule would at least allow a respite during working hours, but clearly that had been too much to hope for.

The sight of Anna had shocked him. Shocked and excited him. The only answer was to drive her away but, hell, it was going to be difficult. He wanted to know who was responsible for making her look so exhausted and vulnerable. He wanted to kiss the bruised-looking smudges around those sapphire-blue eyes. He wanted to know what had gone on with her family, why she wanted no part of her cultural heritage and why she'd had such a financial struggle to achieve her degree. He wanted a magic wand to wave and make the fantasies of the last week possible.

But of course it wasn't possible. He'd known that with absolute certainty so why had he allowed himself the futile indulgence of fantasy? There was no woman in existence that he could allow within the personal barriers he'd been forced to erect. She'd been a sexual reprieve, that was all. How had she put it? A little box, neatly labelled as a holiday fling. That was it exactly.

At least that had been the intention. But Anna Kessel wasn't going to be easily boxed and now Mike had to readjust the perimeters. With a muted groan, he jerked his body away from the door and moved back to his desk. He snatched up the INR result on Molly Smith and stared at it, unseeing.

Was she another Erica Savage? Ambitious? More intent on a career than personal relationships? That was a neat box and one that Mike could understand and accept. But acceptance came only when the rules were followed. His mother had been ambitious but had wanted more than a successful career. Her family had been sacrificed, her children products of an emotional disaster that Mike found unforgivable. No, a meaningful relationship with an ambitious woman was not for him.

And what about the other end of the spectrum? The idea of Anna being a waitress had been no more promising. His ex-fiancée, Tricia, had been a waitress at one time, eager to give up any pretence at a career, depending on him for any decisions and financial support. Even though the financial support had been a struggle in those days Mike had been quite prepared to take on his side of the bargain.

He'd loved Tricia, or thought he had. There had been another important consideration, however. His much younger brother, Nicholas. The commitment to the care of his brother had already been made and hadn't been one Mike had been prepared to relinquish—even for Tricia. He'd thought their love would have been enough for her to accept his brother, to share the responsibility and even, with time, for her to have come to share his love for Nicholas.

They'd gone out. Nicholas hadn't coped well. The drink had been spilled, the food thrown across the table, the chair tipped over. And Nicholas's laugh! The great donkey-like bray which had turned every head in their direction. Tricia had been appalled.

Embarrassed and disgusted. Her reaction had made Mike feel embarrassed as well and he'd been angered by the sense of betrayal it had given him. But it had been more than just being seen in public with a handicapped person for Tricia. She'd told Mike she'd never even consider having his child. What guarantee could there be that his genetic pool wouldn't produce another such monster?

Of course, he tried to enlighten her. Nicholas had been damaged by his premature and difficult birth, prematurity brought on by a mother who refused to modify the workload necessary to maintain her wonderful career. A workload which had made recognition of an unwanted pregnancy too late for easy termination. The unsuccessful, drug-induced attempt had contributed to the early birth of a baby who had survived but who was far from normal.

The relationship dragged on as Mike desperately sought some acceptable compromise but it ended in another emotional disaster when he was dumped in favour of an older man with more on offer and no impediments. Now he was an older man himself and had the resources to conceal the impediment, but there was no attraction in such an unacceptable compromise.

There had been others. Of course there had, but Nicholas had never been exposed to them and Michael Smith's emotional core had been very well protected. Largely untouched, in fact, until he met Anna Kessell. Nobody had ever made him feel like that before. Made him yearn so powerfully for something that he knew to be impossible. And the fantasies! As addictive and futile as those of any teenager. His favourite was that Anna was actually a musician, one of a mysterious breed of artistic person that Mike's experience had not led him to categorise on a personal level. Perhaps the expectations would be different. Perhaps they could be made to accommodate the vision of the overwhelmingly fulfilling relationship he'd allowed himself to dream of.

But Anna wasn't a musician. She wasn't a waitress. She wasn't even a doctor yet, not by his standards anyway. Perhaps if he tried hard enough to antagonise her she'd be glad to escape or retaliate. And then perhaps he'd be able to erase the memory of their night together.

Or at least dampen the awful desire he had to repeat it.

It was the first total hip replacement Anna had witnessed.

She found it all rather horrifying. Scrubbed, gowned and gloved, she stood, feeling like a fifth wheel to one side of Erica who was assisting Mr Smith. The high-pitched whine of the oscillating power saw used to remove the fractured head of the femur had ceased but the silence didn't last. The mallet used to hammer the rasps into the femur to form the hole for the prosthesis was even worse. Erica was doing the hammering with confident enthusiasm and Anna's eyes widened further when Mike picked up what looked like an ordinary cordless drill.

'If you stood somewhere else you might be able to see what was happening, Dr Van Kessel.' The surgeon didn't glance up from his work. 'Then you won't be entirely wasting your time.'

Anna flinched at the sharp tone and moved quickly to the other side of the table. A theatre nurse had to edge sideways to give Anna room in her new position. Erica requested a trial prosthesis to check the size of the hole she'd created.

'I'm about to drill the keying holes into the pelvis,' Mike commented. 'We've already enlarged the acetabulum to fit the prosthetic cup. When we fill these holes with cement, before fitting the cup, the area for adhesion is increased and the joint considerably strengthened.' The sound of the drill precluded any further explanation.

Erica was hammering again and Anna suppressed a wild urge to giggle. It all looked like some bizarre demonstration in a DIY shop. She was reminded of a lecturer in medical school, a physician whose opinion of surgeons had been somewhat prejudiced.

'Some of you will probably aspire to a career in surgery,' he'd told them. 'And some will even attain the dubious honour of giving up your hard-earned title of ''Doctor'' and revert to being ''Mr'' or whatever feminine equivalent you favour.' His opinion of women was also a little biased.

'The distinction arose because physicians originally wouldn't stoop to the performance of such manual procedures as amputations. Surgery was left to the barbers. A doctor was required to do the thinking—a mister was sufficient to do the cutting. It became a tradition that nobody seems to want to change.'

The class had laughed dutifully but Anna had thought at the time that it was doubtful whether she would want to become a surgeon. Now she felt even more doubtful.

'I asked you to pass me the cup.' Mike's tone cut through Anna's reverie. 'Is that a problem, Dr Van Kessel?'

'No—sorry.' Anna turned hurriedly and caught the eye of the theatre nurse she'd displaced earlier. She looked irritated, as though Anna was being deliberately obstructive. The nurse was holding the plastic joint component towards her. Anna reached out to grasp it but the nurse released her hold a fraction early and the cup fell away to bounce against Erica's hand and then onto the floor. There was a moment's appalled silence, then Michael Smith spoke with icy calm.

'I have methyl methacrylate cement about to harden here. I would like a sterile cup available *immediately*!'

Theatre staff moved quickly. Sterile packs were ripped open and Anna stood back as the situation was rectified. It hadn't been entirely her fault but it would certainly be seen as such. She was ignored as the femoral section of the artificial joint was cemented into place and the ball fitted back into the cup. It was left to Erica to patch up the muscle and tendon damage and close the wound. Michael Smith left the theatre without a backward glance at anyone. As the final clearing-up began the theatre nurse came over to Anna.

'I'm sorry about that,' she said. 'It was as much my fault as yours. Things get a bit tense in here sometimes when Mr Smith is operating.'

Erica raised an eyebrow at the nurse but turned back to her suturing. The nurse wasn't deterred. 'What's eating him today, Erica? We thought he'd be at least a little chilled out after two weeks' holiday, but he's grumpier than ever.'

'Hmm.' Erica seemed disinclined to comment. Instead, she looked up at Anna. 'Don't worry, Anna,' she said surprisingly. 'I was as nervous as hell my first time in Theatre. Would you like to do these last sutures?'

Grateful for the friendly overtures, Anna eagerly reached to take the suture needle. Perhaps if she tried to involve herself more enthusiastically she could begin to feel as if she belonged. M.G. Smith's attitude presented an obstacle that only challenged her to overcome it. Maybe if she tried hard enough the barrier he'd erected between them might even begin to crumble. If she could win professional acceptance then maybe—just maybe— something personal would follow.

She'd said that familiarity was the last thing she wanted but part of her knew just how far that really was from the truth. Anna had plenty of time to argue with herself as she changed out of theatre gear and headed back to her ward duties of chasing up test results and paperwork.

Wasn't the humiliation of that final chance meeting enough to have dampened the memory of their night together? Yes, it was, Anna told herself firmly. More than enough. She hadn't just been a 'holiday fling'— she'd been one of a series. She could never degrade herself to the point of finding that acceptable. No wonder Mr Smith was worried about her spreading gossip. It was hardly the type of behaviour one would expect from a consultant surgeon on holiday. Perhaps he was, in fact, leading a double life! The thought was amusing. Maybe it was the possibility of blackmail that was bothering Michael Smith.

If you set out to look for faults it was always easy to find them. Michael Smith found no shortage of examples in Anna's work over the next week. It didn't seem to make any difference how hard she tried. In fact, her efforts often caused more difficulties. Her comprehensive history-taking and delivery were met with exasperation at the time she was taking to relay irrelevant information. When she tried to be more succinct Mr Smith always managed to elicit a piece of information she'd omitted.

'Perhaps you didn't feel it was relevant, Dr Van Kessel. When you have a little more experience you may be able to make a more accurate judgement.'

It didn't matter how many initial diagnostic tests she ordered. Michael Smith would either think of something extra that should have been measured or find cause to berate her over the number she had done.

'Do you have any idea what the laboratory costs are for running tests like these? This department has a budget, Dr Van Kessel, which you seem determined to single-handedly blow out.'

Contact with the head of department's registrar, Ken Slater, and rounds with Tim McPherson were relaxed in comparison, but Anna didn't often get the chance to enjoy them. Frequently, she was expected to be in two places at once, with both consultants seeing a new admission or doing a ward round. Was it because Tim McPherson and Ken were more easygoing that Michael Smith's demands took precedence? Or did Anna just fear more the consequences of not performing up to the expectations of the Smith–Savage team, therefore taking advantage of the other team's willingness to make life a little easier for her?

In any event, the added exposure only served to

inflame the situation and Anna was becoming increasingly miserable. The bone-weariness that dogged her
only accentuated her state of mind. She was never
going to win the professional approval of Michael
Smith. He'd made it his mission to make things as
difficult as possible for her. Did he want her to give
up? To leave? It was certainly a possibility. If nothing
else, perhaps Mr Smith wanted insurance that no gossip would circulate about his private life.

And yet there was more than that to the persecu-
tion. And much more than simply an inability to tolerate fools and a less than warm personality. Eye contact was always as brief as possible, often accidental
but with a frequency that was unnerving. And the
effect each time was just as intense—like being
burned.

Anna felt that Mike was overreacting. It meant that
she was having an effect on him as well. That the
door he'd slammed between them he hadn't been
quite able to lock. Sometimes Anna even had the impression that it was all *her* fault. That she'd hurt him
in some way and he was unable to forgive her.

Initially indignant at the thought, it did, however,
give Anna yet more pause for thought. Watching a
magnificent sunrise during a quiet spell on her next
night on call, Anna recalled their final meeting. OK,
so maybe she had been rude to him but her anger had
been justified. More than justified.

It had been a sunset she'd been watching that day,
not a sunrise, but the colour of the sky had been very
similar and Anna could still recall the sharp pang of
disappointment she'd experienced. The deep rumble
of male voices had made her jump. Her heart thud-

ding, she'd waited for the climbers to join her on the summit of Paku, the little hill dominating the small Coromandel settlement of Tairua. As their heads had appeared some of the tension had left her in a rush. It hadn't been him. With the sunset heralding a cooler temperature, the men hadn't stayed long to admire the view and Anna had soon been left alone again, sitting cross-legged on a large rock.

The sunset was magnificent, a band of cloud behind the jagged outline of Broken Hills illuminated in a fiery glow of red and gold. The name had been well chosen, the peaks distinct from the smoother lines of the ranges that stretched as far as she could see. The toothlike pinnacles only reminded her of Mike. She'd climbed towards them two days ago but her preoccupation with her companion of the night before had detracted considerably from her enjoyment of both the hike and the historical remains.

Just who was he? And why had he simply disappeared like that? It wasn't because he hadn't enjoyed their time together. Quite the opposite. He'd seemed as overwhelmed and thankful for the experience as Anna had been. She kept looking for him, hoping each time she heard voices on the path that he might suddenly appear. The track was a popular one and she had several disappointments.

She'd thought she'd spotted his tent in the camping ground at Pauanui yesterday and had made far more trips to the washing and cooking facilities than she'd required, hoping to catch a glimpse of the occupant. Even the later shopping expedition had done nothing to distract her. It was because of Mike that she'd been forced to purchase a new bathing suit. She hadn't even returned to the swimming hole to try and find her old one. In the changing room she'd experienced a vivid flash of memory, reliving the wave of excitement as the straps of her worn bathing suit had been eased off her shoulders—the sensation of freedom as her breasts had been released from the tight, confining fabric—the touch of his hands as he—

'Are you all right in there?'

Anna blushed scarlet, hoping desperately she hadn't moaned aloud as the sales assistant poked her head through the curtain.

'It—it seems a good fit,' she said quickly.

'Mmm. The colour's perfect.' They both admired the sapphire-blue suit in the full-length mirror. 'It's exactly the same colour as your eyes. Have you got tinted contact lenses?'

'No.' Anna sighed. Why did some people assume that her good features couldn't possibly be natural?

The girl sighed as well. 'Some people have all the luck. Do you want to take the togs?'

'Yes. I'll just wear them, thanks. I'm going for a swim.' Anna saw the assistant eyeing her figure and reached for her T-shirt before the girl could query whether her breast size might be due to surgical augmentation. The shaping of the cups certainly did nothing to hide that particular asset. What if she met Mike on the beach? Would it make him regret simply walking out on her like that?

He wasn't on the beach and by this morning Anna had been finally convinced she'd never see the man again. The disappointment wouldn't be tinged by anger or regret, she decided. It had been a night of pure magic, a memory she could treasure for the rest of her life. Now it was time to move on.

Anna treated herself to a day trip, travelling up the

coast on a jet boat to Cathedral Cove, which had to
be the most beautiful beach she had ever seen. The
sharp slope of the coast and the depth of the sea right
to the shoreline made the sea an impressively dark
blue. The sand was a pure white and the edges of the
beach shaded by the gnarled trunks and deep green
foliage of ancient Pohutukawa trees. The beach was
divided by the amazing rock formation that gave the
cove its name and the day was perfect. Well, almost
perfect.

With a sigh, Anna clambered down from her rock.
It was now nearly dark, the colour draining the sky
to shades of pink and pale gold, and the boats in the
channel becoming dark blobs as the final fingers of
sunlight gilded the water around them.

Anna hurried down the silent, leaf-lined track past
huge, mossy boulders. It was too dark and isolated
for her to be alone here. Mike would have told her
she was mad and he'd probably have been right. With
relief Anna passed the sign that informed would-be
climbers to keep their dogs on leashes because it was
kiwi territory, and found herself back on the footpath
and among the gardens and houses of the Paku resi-
dents. A brisk walk down the hill brought her to the
jetty for the brief ride across to Pauanui.

Anna took her boots off for her final walk along
the beach back to the camping ground. She was due
to finish her holiday the next day and head back to
Tauranga to begin work. She wanted to savour these
last moments of leisure. A beach party was in full
swing nearby, a large group of people enjoying a
driftwood fire and barbecue.

Anna's attention was caught by the high-pitched
voice of a statuesque blonde.

'It's just *too* hot! I'm going for a swim!'

Anna's eyes widened as the woman stepped out of her white dress. The matching bikini beneath was minuscule—just strings with a few strategically placed patches, gleaming against the dark tan of an impressive body. Anna frowned, not at the blatant exposure but at the way the woman lurched slightly as she began to run.

'Come with me, darling!' the woman shrieked happily. 'Last one in's a rotten egg!'

'Darling' didn't make himself immediately available. In fact, the woman was apparently being ignored by the party-goers. The noisy buzz of conversation and laughter continued unabated and no heads turned to watch either her disrobing or her move towards the surf. Anna hesitated. The party-goer was probably only intending to dampen the brightly painted toenails but in case she really intended swimming someone had better watch her. She'd clearly had too much to drink to be able to swim safely.

Sure enough, the blonde kept going. At waist depth a large wave came in as she turned to wave excitedly at the party and she was knocked over. Anna waited for her to surface, her scanning becoming more concentrated as the seconds ticked by. When the blonde head became visible it was well behind the line of the breakers in a calm patch of water which indicated a potential rip. Anna peeled off her sweatshirt and dropped it on top of her boots. She yelled to attract attention to the situation as she began to run.

The rip was a strong one and Anna was thankful that her active holiday had bumped up her fitness level. She was also thankful that the blonde woman was virtually unconscious and unable to struggle ef-

fectively as she towed her back to shore. A strong
pair of hands reached out beside Anna in the shallow
surf and the woman was lifted and then laid in a limp
heap on the sand. Anna reached out to take her pulse
but her hand was brushed aside.

'I'll do that.'

Anna gasped. Looking up, she found herself staring
at Mike but he was intent on the prone figure before
him. Anna backed off as more party-goers began to
crowd around them, several holding towels and chat-
tering nervously. The blonde woman suddenly moved
convulsively, struggled to a half-sitting position, vom-
ited and then began crying noisily. Anna turned away.
The rescue had been successful and 'darling' was
clearly available to take over the supervision.

Nobody offered Anna a towel and she was shivering as she pulled her sweatshirt back on. She bent
to retrieve her boots.

'Well done,' said a quiet voice behind her. 'I suppose lifesaving is something else you're quite good
at.'

Anna straightened. Her emotions were in turmoil
from the tension of the rescue and the shock of seeing
Mike again when she'd finally stopped expecting it.
He looked quite calm—as though completely used to
chance meetings with women with whom he'd recently shared a night of tumultuous passion. His expression angered Anna. For the first time she felt as
though she'd been used. Used—and discarded. Her
anger warmed her and she stopped shivering.

'You seem to make a habit of hanging out with wet
women,' she said acidly. 'Why don't you tell your
bimbo friend that swimming after excessive amounts
of alcohol isn't a good idea?'

Mike's mouth tightened. It made it easy to forget just how soft and mobile those lips could be. 'You seem to be making quite a few assumptions here, Anna. I should have thought that the label of "bimbo" would be one you would be particularly careful of.'

'Somebody who advertises that blatantly wants assumptions to be made,' Anna snapped. 'But I'm sure you're aware of that. In case you were wondering, her hair colour is far from natural and she's definitely hunting for a man. You'd better get back. Time must be precious on one-night stands.'

His tone was dangerously quiet. 'Is that what you think you were?'

'Yes.' Anna gave Mike a direct stare. 'What else could I possibly think, having been walked out on? You didn't even bother to say goodbye or to thank me for a good time.' Her voice hardened. 'I'm assuming it *was* a good time, of course.'

Mike turned and looked out to sea. Behind them, the group had bundled the bimbo into towels and was ushering her back towards the fire. Their concerned voices had faded before Mike spoke again.

'I left like that because I wanted nothing to spoil the memory of what had been an extraordinary night,' he said softly. 'Perfect, in fact. There was no way it could be continued. I didn't want an uncomfortable parting or empty promises made.'

'Oh, I see.' Anna thought she understood perfectly. 'You wanted to put it in a little box, neatly labelled as a holiday fling.'

'What else could it be?' Mike spoke harshly. 'I knew it was extremely unlikely that we'd ever meet

again. I'm sorry we have. I'm sorry I'll have to remember your low opinion of me.'

'You'll get over it.' Holding her boots by the laces,
Anna began to walk away. 'I'll have no trouble for-
getting. I suppose it's all part of one-night-stand eti-
quette—not even telling someone your surname.' She
walked faster.

'It's Smith!' The call from behind sounded more
like a curse, but Anna had laughed with genuine
amusement.

'Pull the other one, Mike,' she shouted sarcastically
over her shoulder. 'It's got bells on it!'

CHAPTER FOUR

No.

Mike had no right to blame her simply for spoiling a pleasurable memory for him. And even if he did it was very unprofessional of him to punish her through his new position of advantage. At least she was mature enough to separate the issues. With difficulty Anna had managed to avoid any retaliation by keeping an iron control of her temper. Any swearing had been strictly silent. She was in no position to confront Michael Smith on either a professional or personal level. And she had to admit that some of the reprimands were justified. He had an amazing knack of finding her doing something she shouldn't be doing.

Anna found the pleasures in her job were increasingly few and far between. The moments that were enjoyable she tended to welcome and make the most of. Many of them were found on the paediatric ward. Anna discovered that Michael Smith had an international reputation for his work with handicapped children. The results of his surgical intervention to improve mobility and quality of life for children with handicaps such as spina bifida and cerebral palsy led to many children being referred to Tauranga from other centres. She learned that his private practice dealt exclusively with such cases and that one day a week he spent in Auckland, running a similar clinic for those who could not travel to see him.

'I don't know why he works in a peripheral centre,'

Erica had told her. 'He would be snapped up by any specialist hospital anywhere in the world with far greater potential for advancement.' Erica had shaken her head. She simply could not understand his apparent lack of ambition. Neither did she share Michael Smith's interest in disabled children. But Anna did.

The positive and caring atmosphere of the paediatric ward made Anna feel more at home than anywhere else in the hospital. She knew she spent too much time in there and that it increased the pressure and potential for errors in her other duties, but she simply couldn't resist it. It was unfortunate that Michael Smith had caught her during her admission of Emily Jacobs.

It was a straightforward admission, the history already well documented. Emily was a two-and-a-half-year-old girl with severe spina bifida. She was being admitted to undergo treatment for her dislocated hips which would then allow her to learn to walk with the aid of callipers. Emily was delightful. She wasn't intimidated in the least by being hospitalised yet again. Her bright eyes were shining at the prospect of the wealth of available toys and playmates and her contagious gurgles of laughter were very easily elicited. Anna had her in paroxsyms of mirth by using a small, furry, toy mouse.

She had her hand under the cover of the bed and the lump she made was twitching. 'Look out, Emily—here he comes!'

The child shrieked with delight as the lump made forays closer to her paralysed legs.

'He might bite your toe!'

More shrieks and Emily swiped happily towards the lump she couldn't reach. Anna slowed down the progress of the mouse and Emily grew quiet as it approached the top. There was a long pause with the lump only an inch away from exposure. Emily's eyes widened and her mouth dropped open in excited anticipation. Suddenly Anna shot the mouse out of its covering and then pulled it under again just as quickly. Emily squealed with glee and they both collapsed in giggles.

It was only then that Anna became aware of the observers at the end of Emily's bed. Michael Smith stood with the senior paediatric nurse who was laughing. The expression on Mr Smith's face was strange but certainly couldn't be considered amused. He was wearing theatre greens and avoided eye contact with Anna, who scrambled to an upright position and tried to catch the wisps of long hair that had worked loose from the neatly pinned knot at her nape.

'I take it you've completed Emily's admission?' Mike was staring at Anna's hastily scribbled notes lying askew on the end of the bed. The mouse game had displaced two sheets of notepaper. Anna bent to retrieve them from the floor.

'Yes. I'll write them up now.'

'And have you also completed the admission for Todd Marshall?'

'No, not yet.' Todd was another disabled child being admitted for corrective surgery, this time to his feet.

'I'll be in to see him in a minute. Perhaps you could attend to his admission details before I get there.'

'Of course.' Anna smiled at Emily. The toddler's happy demeanour had faded with the consultant's tone of voice. Anna could see a hint of anxiety in the wide blue eyes. Quickly she reached under the bed cover and produced the mouse. Emily's face lit up again.

'Look after him for me, sweetheart,' Anna whispered, 'but make sure he doesn't bite your toes.'

Emily giggled and Anna reached for her stethoscope, also lying discarded on the end of the bed.

'I came to discuss the details of surgery with Mrs Jacobs,' Michael Smith said. 'Where is she?'

'She had to go in to work for a few hours,' Anna explained. Emily's mother had been a pleasure to talk to. It was easy to see why the child was so happy. Sue Jacobs managed a difficult parenting job at the same time as holding down a part-time secretarial position. 'She'll be back this afternoon.'

'I should hope so. Unfortunately I won't be available to talk to her at that time.'

Anna was angered by his attitude. Surely he knew that Sue Jacobs depended on her job. The added tension of a disabled child had been enough to cause the break-up of her marriage. Sue struggled to make ends meet and found the forced separation from her daughter very difficult. Anna's control of her temper slipped a notch. 'Mrs Jacobs has arranged several days off for the time of Emily's surgery,' she informed Mike coolly. 'There were some loose ends that she had to tie up this morning. She can't afford to lose her job.'

'You seem to have a lot of time for in-depth socialising with your patients' relatives, Dr Van Kessel. I suggest you use your time a little more constructively with the duties that you are responsible for. Like admitting Todd Marshall.' The tawny eyes inflicted a searing glance and Anna felt a now familiar tingle down her spine and a tightness deep within her. It didn't override the irritation she felt and she stalked off. He hadn't even said hello to Emily, and if a patient's social circumstances weren't part of her responsibility then they jolly well should be!

It was even more unfortunate that it had been the same day that Michael Smith had found her in another favourite spot, Room 6 of the orthopaedic ward. Room 6 had four occupants, all young men. They were all victims of car and motorbike accidents and the severity of their injuries meant they had been— or would be—in hospital for a considerable length of time. They intended to enjoy their incarceration and took delight in making the most of any contact with the female staff.

Nurses, physios, X-ray technicians and kitchen staff were all appreciated, but Anna was now a great favourite and the lads generally cheered whenever she appeared. Having got over her initial embarrassment at her popularity, Anna now took pleasure in stopping to chat for a few minutes when the opportunity arose.

The most recent admission to Room 6 was Tony McLaughlin. Horrifically injured when his motorbike had collided with a furniture truck, eighteen-year-old Tony had already spent two weeks in Intensive Care. The halo traction he was in wasn't sufficient to stabilise the neck fracture he'd received and his general condition had now improved enough for transfer to the ward and probable further surgery. Anna liked Tony. His cheerful determination to recover despite the odds against him were inspiring, and she looked forward to her daily call to update his status. This time there was something new to comment on.

'Whose guitar is that, Tony?'

'Mine. I asked Mum to bring it in.'

Anna looked at her patient. He was flat on his back,

his legs paralysed and only limited movement and feeling in his arms. A mirror was positioned to one side of his pillow to increase his field of view.

'It's beautiful.' Anna leaned closer. 'Wow, it's a Martin! Awesome!'

'You know guitars.' Tony sounded pleasantly surprised. 'I saved for three years to buy that.'

'It's gorgeous.' Anna touched the shiny woodwork. 'May I?' Her hand closed around the neck of the instrument.

'Sure.' Tony winked, his immobilised equivalent of a nod.

Anna perched on the end of the bed. 'I've dreamed of a Martin,' she told Tony. 'A twelve-string but they're way out of my price range.'

'Are you into classical?'

'Yeah.' Anna was automatically tuning the guitar. 'Me, too.'

Anna tightened a string fractionally. For someone as passionate about an instrument as Tony must have been to pour his savings into a top-of-the-range model, his present condition must be heartbreaking. To distract both Tony and herself from a depressing train of thought, Anna launched into the opening bars of 'Duelling Banjos'.

Tony grinned. 'Cool!'

'It's better on a banjo,' Anna admitted. 'Two banjos, actually.' But her rapid-fire plucking drew cheers from the other lads. Suddenly she stopped. 'Damn, I've broken my nail. Do you have any picks?'

'Try the case,' Tony suggested.

It didn't help that Anna had put down the guitar when Michael Smith entered Room 6. The big doors were wide open and he must have heard what had been going on. He looked furious.

'One of these days, Dr Van Kessel, you may surprise me by actually attending to some of your medical duties. I have just wasted a considerable period of time trying to locate Molly Smith's notes. I'm now told they were last seen in your possession.'

'Oops!' Anna took the set of notes from the end of Tony's bed. 'Sorry. I was just about to put them back. I had to write up my notes on her new ECG. She's been getting a bit of chest pain.'

'Patient conditions and their notes are confidential. You do not leave notes lying around unattended and you do not discuss their status in front of other patients.'

Anna sighed. If she hadn't mentioned Molly's new symptom no doubt she'd have been guilty of not following up a significant problem. She followed the consultant out of Room 6 after an apologetic smile at Tony.

'The ECG's unchanged,' she said. 'No sign of an MI.'

'There are other considerations for chest pain,' Mike said brusquely. 'Especially in a seventy-four-year-old woman who's recently had major surgery.'

Anna nodded. Molly was five days post-surgery now and had been mobilising well, keen to get home and rescue Blossom from Elaine's supposedly less than ideal level of care. Anna couldn't blame her for being suspicious. She'd met Molly's neighbour during a visiting hour. Another elderly woman, Elaine had confided in Anna that her canine charge was proving disruptive.

'If I wasn't so fond of Molly I wouldn't have the

thing in my house,' she'd whispered, out of Molly's earshot. 'When it isn't yapping or refusing to eat anything I produce it just sits and glares at me with these poppy little eyes. I'm sure it's trying to decide which ankle to sink its nasty, sharp teeth into.'

'Molly really appreciates you taking care of Blossom,' Anna had responded. 'It's a wonderful thing to be doing for her and it will help her recovery enormously not having to worry.'

But Molly didn't even mention Blossom when Anna trailed in Mike's wake to revisit her patient. Her condition had deteriorated even in the hour since Anna had checked her and Molly was now quite short of breath and looking distressed. Erica was summoned and Anna was kept busy helping with the repeat ECG, arterial blood sample, chest X-ray and other investigations rapidly ordered. When a pulmonary embolism was deemed the most likely diagnosis Erica began drug treatment with an anticoagulant, ordered urgent pulmonary angiography and initiated the now necessary cardiovascular support with drugs and oxygen.

The emergency was time-consuming and Anna had to work on well into the evening to ensure she'd seen all her patients and updated the reports. At least it wasn't a night on call. By the time she made it to the cafeteria the only available meal was the understandably unpopular macaroni cheese.

Halfway through the unappetising meal Anna had the horrible thought that she hadn't returned Molly Smith's notes to the appropriate trolley. Abandoning her dinner, she raced back to the ward. Visiting hour was finishing and she smiled at the noise level from

Room 6. It looked like a whole football team had gone to cheer up one of Tony's companions.

Tony, however, was alone. After checking that she had, in fact, replaced Molly's notes, Anna decided to pop in to see Tony. With their shared love for guitar music she felt closer to the young man. He was also facing major surgery within the next few days with no guarantee that it would improve his long-term prospects. Anna's sympathies were strongly aroused.

Pausing to brush her hair in the staff toilet, Anna impulsively decided not to tie it back again. She then removed her white coat and draped it over her arm. She was off duty now, thank goodness.

The inhabitants of Room 6 were effusively welcoming. They hadn't seen her before without the shapeless white coat or without the magnificent curtain of silky hair tied firmly back. The clinging scoop-necked top and softly gathered floral skirt with flowers as blue as her eyes made a picture feminine enough to stir any young male. The colour and length of her unrestrained hair made her seem younger and even more desirable. One youth managed a very suggestive wolf whistle but Anna only grinned.

'You've had more than enough visitors for one night, Malcolm,' she told him. 'I just came to see Tony for a minute.' She caught Tony's eye in his mirror as she sat in the chair beside his bed. 'How's it going?'

The young man was silent for a moment, then he sighed. 'I asked Mum to bring my guitar in, you know? I keep thinking that maybe, after the operation, I'll be able to use my hands well enough to play again.'

Anna nodded. She could hear the fear in his voice. 'I hope so, too, Tony, I really do.'

'Even if I was in a wheelchair for the rest of my life, it wouldn't be so bad if I could still play, you know?'

Anna nodded again. 'I think I'd feel the same way.'

'Yeah.' Tony's gaze in the mirror was intense. 'You're probably the only person who really understands.' He cleared his throat, struggling for emotional control. 'Play something for me?' he asked quietly. 'I'd really like to hear it even if I can't play just yet.'

'Sure.' Anna willingly picked up the guitar. She couldn't help checking the tuning again.

'Yo! Mr Smith!'

Anna glanced up at Malcolm's call, aware of a sinking sensation at the consultant's entrance. She tried to dismiss the feeling that she had no right to be there. This was her time, one of a very few precious hours in her present existence when she could do as she chose. So what if there was some regulation about social contact with patients that she was contravening. Anna was annoyed to even have to consider it. But Michael Smith said nothing. His eyes met Anna's with the intensity she was growing accustomed to but his attention was elsewhere.

'Hello, Malcolm.' The surgeon walked past Tony's bed. 'I came to see how that new skin graft is taking.'

'Pretty good, I think, Doc. That plastic surgeon looked pleased with it this morning.' Malcolm waved a hand at his leg, suspended in a canvas sling. The extensive exterior fixation which had been required for the multiple and compound fractures made the limb look as if it belonged to a robot rather than a human. Metal bars were held in place with numerous long pins that protruded at various angles. 'It's a funny shape, though.'

'You lost a lot of muscle,' Mike told him. 'It was touch and go whether you could even keep the leg— as you know. Some of it is wastage. If the skin graft is ready we'll get you up and make a start on some weight-bearing. The bone union is looking excellent on today's X-rays.'

Mike's comments faded as Tony whispered to Anna, 'He's a pretty good surgeon, isn't he?'

'Sure is,' Anna replied sincerely. 'From what I've heard, he's quite famous internationally.'

'I guess I'm lucky.' Tony's mouth quirked. 'Pity he's such a grumpy sod.'

Anna bit back a smile. 'What would you like me to play?'

'Play something for Mr Smith—put him in a good mood before he starts talking about my operation.'

'OK.' Anna's smile escaped. 'How 'bout this?' She played and sang the opening of Carly Simon's 'You're so Vain'. Catching Tony's eye in the mirror, she saw he was laughing. Without thinking, Anna glanced up further and the words to the song died on her lips at the expression on Michael Smith's face. She cleared her throat. 'Right. Let's be serious about this.' Anna bent her head, was silent for a moment, then began a soft plucking that invited careful listening.

Mike had to escape. Taking Malcolm's notes, he retreated to the corridor but then could go no further. He leaned against the wall opposite one of the large windows on either side of the doors into Room 6. The curtains hadn't yet been drawn for the night and he had a clear view of Anna, sitting beside Tony's bed, her face screened by the golden fall of hair that swung slowly to the rhythm of the music.

The song she was singing was Roberta Flack's 'Killing Me Softly'. A haunting enough tune in itself, the skilful playing and Anna's beautiful voice carried through the ward as she lost herself in the song and forgot to be self-conscious. Mobile patients began to appear in the corridor, to stand and listen as Mike was doing. Staff slowed and some stopped completely, one with a full bedpan in her hand, mesmerised by the unusual and striking occurrence.

Mike was more than mesmerised. The words and the emotion they carried cut him to the quick. The emotional spell Anna was casting had him floundering helplessly in its web. He'd never experienced anything that had touched his soul this deeply—except, perhaps, the night he'd spent with Anna Kessel. He saw tears escape and fall down young Tony McLaughlin's cheek and knew exactly how the lad felt. A recognition of one's own needs—a desperate longing to somehow put things right even when a solution seemed only a fantasy.

The verse ended and the final chorus began. Singing more softly now, Anna raised her head. She looked directly at Mike and the obstacle of a window between them was no shelter. The connection was there and could no longer be denied. Mike didn't even try to look away. He knew, with absolute certainty, that he and Anna had to be together. Even though Anna's expression didn't change and her voice didn't falter, he could see in her eyes an acceptance of the same knowledge.

The only question now was where. And when.

With characteristically decisive movements Michael Smith strode through the applause Anna's performance had elicited. He handed Malcolm's notes to a passing nurse with a curt instruction to replace them. He continued on towards his office.

Anna was just leaving the ward when a nurse called to her. 'There's a phone call for you Anna. On line two. Sounds like ''Jaws''.'

'Oh, God, what have I done now?' Anna muttered. Perhaps it was to inform her that regulations governing the duties of house surgeons specifically excluded impromptu concerts.

'Anna Kessel.'

'I need to talk to you, Anna. Privately.' The tone was tense. It didn't invite a response. 'Be at the side entrance in ten minutes. I'll pick you up in my car.' A short silence and then, more softly, 'Please.'

Anna had no time to respond before the line went dead. Dazed, she put the receiver down slowly. What if she simply refused to jump at his command, refused to give him the opportunity to say whatever he had on his mind? That would certainly go a long way to putting M.G. Smith in his place. But Anna knew she wouldn't refuse. She was facing a turning-point in their relationship and she knew exactly what direction she had to take.

It *was* a black BMW.

The sleek machine cruised to a halt beside Anna. The passenger door swung open and Anna climbed in, feeling a little ridiculous.

'I feel like I've stepped into a spy movie,' she told Mike. 'What's with all this cloak-and-dagger, hiding-at-the-side-entrance business? And what happened to the red Porsche?'

The car moved off as soon as Anna closed the door. She hurriedly fastened her seat belt.

'The Porsche was rented,' Mike told her calmly. 'I felt like a change. As for wanting our meeting to be discreet, a private relationship between a consultant and a junior member of staff is not the type of gossip I wish to have associated with myself.'

'We haven't got a private relationship,' Anna pointed out. 'If you're inferring that I've said something about our brief acquaintanceship to anybody then you're mistaken.' Her tone became defensive. 'Where would I find the time to gossip, even if I wanted to? Not that I expect you to believe me,' she added bitterly. 'You've made it very clear that nothing I do meets with your approval.'

The car left the hospital grounds and picked up speed. 'I have been hard on you,' Mike admitted. 'But if it's any consolation it hasn't been entirely personal. I'm hard on all junior staff.'

'So I've heard,' muttered Anna.

'Oh?' The glance directed at Anna was brief but vaguely amused. 'What is it that the rank and file have to say about me?'

Anna took a gulp of air. The close proximity and totally new situation she found herself in was unnerving. The tension in the car was palpable but she knew it had nothing to do with the conversation. It was a sexual tension, created by whatever chemistry existed between them. A chemistry that was rapidly approaching meltdown. She tried to laugh.

'They call you "Jaws".'

'Why? Do I eat too much?' The car was leaving

the city behind, the route leading them over one of the harbour bridges and towards the vast sweep of Ocean and Papamoa beaches that stretched away from the distinctive cone of Mount Maunganui.

'No. You take chunks out of people when they least expect it.'

Mike laughed and the tension ebbed just a little. 'They should expect it by now. I told you I'm not good at tolerating fools. People either learn fast, working for me, or they find employment elsewhere.'

'That's exactly what I've been considering,' Anna said quietly. 'It's not much comfort to know that I'm not the only one suffering or that it's a bid to create a constructive learning environment on your part. Do you have any idea just how miserable you've made my working hours?' Not to mention all the other hours, she added silently. Restless hours that never seemed to deal adequately with the emotional turbulence.

Mike pulled the BMW into a parking slot overlooking Ocean beach. He killed the engine, unclipped his safety belt and directed his whole attention to his passenger. Anna felt the internal knot tighten painfully. The barrier was down. This was the real person she was finally seeing. The memory of passion surged through her and made her pulse race.

'It was bad enough meeting you and knowing we would never meet again,' Mike said in a low voice. 'Seeing you every day and knowing nothing could come of it was unbearable.' His voice strengthened. 'I was trying to drive you away, Anna, and I apologise. On a professional level it was inexcusable. On a personal level…' Mike paused and cleared his throat. 'It was entirely unsuccessful.' There was a long pause which Anna was incapable of breaking. When Mike spoke again his voice was husky. 'I want you, Anna Kessel. I...I need you. But I doubt that I can offer you what you might want in a relationship.'

Anna could sense how difficult it was for Mike to admit his need. Making himself vulnerable was clearly an alien experience. What did he mean by not being able to offer her what she wanted? All she wanted—all she could feel at that point was the desperate need for his touch. To find out whether reality could possibly match a much cherished memory. Her hand was shaking as she unclipped her own seat belt. Her voice was as husky as his.

'I want you, too,' was all she could say.

The kiss was more than she remembered, more than even fantasy could conjure. More—but not nearly enough. Eagerly, Anna twisted her body, encouraging Mike's hand to slip inside the soft cotton top. Her own hand felt the dark fabric of the suit trousers, slid over it until the upward direction was halted by his frustrated groan.

'This is impossible, Anna.' He let go of her and started the engine. 'Where do you live?'

'In the house-surgeons' quarters at the hospital.'

Mike stared at her in disbelief and cut the engine again. 'That's hopeless,' he muttered. 'I can't allow us to be seen together at the hospital.'

Anna accepted that. She wouldn't want the general knowledge or the associated gossip herself and it could only be compounded by Mike being in the position he was.

'Where do you live?' she queried, but Mike's head-shake was violent.

'Out of the question, unfortunately.'

'Why, are you married or something?' The question popped out before Anna could stop it. The flash of anger she saw in Mike's eyes frightened her. His tone was cold.

'Do you really think that's likely?'

'I have no idea,' Anna said shakily. 'For all I know you might lead a double life. A successful surgeon with a respected position in society, a wonderful house with a wife and children to match on the one hand...'

'And on the other?' Mike was staring at Anna and she smiled nervously in response. It had to be said some time.

'On the other a holiday Casanova with a flashy red Porsche and a line-up of blonde bimbos.'

Mike sighed but the sigh became a wry chuckle. 'Quite an appealing scenario but quite inaccurate, I'm afraid. I can see how you might have arrived at the idea. The Porsche was merely a diversion. I had this car in for servicing and decided to try something different. My attendance at that beach party was a mistake. I was persuaded to go by some acquaintances I bumped into. I had never met the ''bimbo'' you rescued and never saw her again, thank goodness. I was angry at finding myself in an unattractive situation but I was more angry at you for drawing an obvious assumption. I suppose I ought to apologise again.'

'Well, I was pretty rude to you myself,' Anna conceded. 'It must be rather insulting not to have your name taken seriously. Let's just forget it.'

'For the record, Anna, I'm not married and I'm not ''or something'' either. And I don't want to forget all of it,' Mike murmured. 'There's one part I particularly enjoy remembering.'

Anna found the distance between them closing again but she wasn't sure who was moving. 'Me, too,' she whispered.

The ringing of the cellphone was intrusive. Mike's clipped tones between the short silences destroyed the atmosphere of impending intimacy.

'What are the blood gases like?' Pause. 'She's very hypoxic. What's her level of consciousness?' Pause. 'What about the other bloods? Have you ruled out sepsis?' Pause. 'Has the pulmonary angiogram been done?' Pause.

'Contact Cardiology. We'll have to start some thrombolytics. Streptokinase. No, Orthopaedics is no place to monitor the administration. Try and get her into ICU. She'll need monitoring for oxygenation as well. And see what Cardiology says about an urgent catheterisation to break up the clot. And we'll have to think about an ultrasound. DVT in a femoral vein is another possibility. I'll be there myself shortly.' Mike pushed down the aerial of the phone with a snap. 'I've got to get back to the hospital. Molly Smith is deteriorating.'

They drove in silence. Anna found herself wondering why Mike's home circumstances precluded a visit from her. She felt instinctively that it was a private area he wasn't yet ready to share with her. But she believed him when he said he wasn't married or attached in some way. Right now, the priority had to be the way they felt about each other. Surely there was some way they could be together. Suddenly Anna chuckled.

'What's funny?'

'I just had a vision of us checking into a motel,' she responded. 'Registering as Mr and Mrs Smith.'

Mike drew to a halt near the outside entrance of the hospital wing that contained the house-surgeons' quarters. 'Can't you move out of the hospital? Find a flat somewhere?'

'I'm on call every second night,' Anna reminded him. 'When I'm not on call I'm too tired to even think. There's no way I could even look for a place.'

Mike nodded grimly. 'I'm doing something about that. I've told management they'll have to roster general surgical staff for cover. I'm not having my juniors too exhausted to function properly—for the patients' sakes as well as their own. You should be down to a one in four roster by next week.'

'Thanks,' Anna said gratefully. 'That should make life a lot more tolerable. But it doesn't solve this particular problem.'

'Why not?'

'Because even if I found a place I couldn't afford it,' Anna admitted reluctantly. Then she chuckled again. 'I guess I could always find a part-time waitressing job again.'

Mike wasn't amused. His look became even more annoyed when his cellphone rang again.

'I've already told you I'm on my way, Ken,' he snapped.

Anna climbed out of the car which glided rapidly away. Because of the tinted windows she wasn't sure whether Mike had smiled or even waved at her, but it didn't matter. Anna felt happy despite her physical frustration. The turning-point had come and gone. It was an astonishingly great relief to find that the direction in which she wanted to go was apparently available. It was simply a question of logistics and surely a solution to that difficulty could be found.

* * *

Molly Smith died during the night. Anna was dismayed at this unexpectedly depressing start to the day. She'd hoped that the change between herself and Mike would somehow make her working environment more enjoyable and fulfilling. Molly's death was a blow—one that she didn't have time to try and come to terms with. It was even more upsetting to find Molly's neighbour, Elaine, on the ward, collecting Molly's belongings. The elderly woman was in tears.

'I was the closest thing to family Molly had. We've been neighbours for thirty years.'

'I'm very sorry,' Anna said. 'You must have been very good friends.'

'We had our differences.' Elaine blew her nose noisily. 'I was never very kind about Blossom. I suppose I was a bit jealous.'

'What will you do about Blossom?'

Elaine looked surprised. 'I'll keep her, of course. She's all I have left to remind me of Molly. And she's quite a sweet little thing, really.'

Anna was called to see Tony as Elaine left. He was feeling awful and his temperature and heart rate were significantly up. Anna took some bloods and sent them off for urgent analysis. She hoped it wasn't the start of an infection that would delay the surgery to his neck and complicate the recovery from his other injuries.

The delays had been unexpected. Due in Theatre at 8 a.m., Anna arrived at a breathless run to find she was the last to get ready and scrubbed.

'Kind of you to join us, Doctor,' Mike said sarcastically. 'Perhaps we can get started now.'

The patient was little Emily Jacobs. Anna had to look away as Mike made the sweeping incision from the top of the hip down to mid-thigh level on the tiny plump leg. Her eye was caught by the object on top of the anaesthesia equipment. A furry toy mouse. The anaesthetist saw her eyes widen.

'I had to put her to sleep before she'd let go of it,' he told Anna. 'I hope it doesn't get lost.'

'I'll take care of it,' Anna promised.

'Perhaps we can take care of some of your training, Dr Kessel.' Anna jumped at being noticed by Mike. She moved in towards the table and tried to concentrate. 'The congenital paralytic dislocation of the hips that Emily has is caused by muscle imbalance. Do you know why that causes dislocation?'

'Um... The hip is pulled into a position in which the head of the femur isn't well covered by the acetabulum.'

'Correct. In Emily's case we have strong adductors with weak abductors and the head has dislocated laterally. The dislocation is easy enough to reduce but it would be pointless unless we can correct the muscle imbalance. I've just detached the anterior third of the iliac crest with the associated abdominal muscles here. You can see the inner and outer surfaces of the ilium.'

Anna peered more closely at the open wound. She watched Mike and Erica work, ligating and dividing blood vessels and tracing the path of the iliopsoas tendon.

'Smillie knife, thanks,' Mike ordered. 'We'll detach the lesser trochanter.'

Anna watched in fascination as a hole was made in the wing of the ilium and the whole of the iliacus and the iliopsoas tendon was passed through the hole.

'Quarter-inch burr,' Mike requested.

It was much easier to become involved from the anatomical perspective. Anna could almost forget that it was a small girl with an infectious giggle and a fondness for furry mice. Almost. She was impressed with the engineering of muscles and tendons that she was watching. The lesser trochanter with its attached psoas tendon was drawn forward through the new hole Mike had pierced through the greater trochanter. Erica was suturing this attachment under tension.

Mike nodded with satisfaction then his attention flicked back to Anna. 'You need a range of hip abduction of at least sixty per cent so that the tendon can be properly attached to the greater trochanter under tension. If it's less than that you have to release the adductor tendon first.'

'Emily had that done two weeks ago, didn't she?'

Mike nodded. 'Suture the origin of the iliacus to the gluteal aspect of the ilium now, Erica. No—further over. That's right. Then you can reattach the iliac crest and close up.' Mike stepped back from the table. 'We'll do an iliopsoas transfer on her other hip in another two weeks. We don't want to immobilise her for any longer than absolutely necessary. It's a major cause of pathological fractures—immobility.'

Anna nodded and then caught Mike's gaze directly for the first time that morning. His tone had been as coolly professional as ever, his sarcastic comment on her late arrival as unpleasant as ever. But there was one big difference and the fact that only his eyes were visible above the mask only served to accentuate it. The anger was gone. The intensity of the gaze was still enough to have a peculiar effect on Anna's abdominal muscles but it was an effect she could savour for the first time, instead of flinching away from it.

Anna glanced away, sure that some signal would transmit itself to the rest of the theatre staff if their eye contact continued.

'Do I need to stay scrubbed?' she queried.

Mike was stripping off his gloves. 'Any problems on the ward?'

'Tony's running a temperature. I need to chase up the bloods I took on him. There's a couple of booked admissions coming in this morning and I'm sure a few more things have cropped up by now.'

'You'd better get back, then. Shame. There's an emergency internal fixation for a complicated compound fracture coming in next. You'd have found it interesting.'

Anna smiled beneath her mask. He made it sound almost like a date. 'Maybe next time.' She pulled off her own gloves and headed towards the doors.

'Haven't you forgotten something, Dr Kessel?'

Anna turned sharply at the brusque query. Erica paused in her final suturing and stared at her. Anna felt confused. She hadn't touched a thing. What could she possibly have done wrong this time?

'Emily's mouse,' Michael Smith announced clearly. 'I believe you offered to take responsibility for it.'

The laughter that rippled through the theatre was muted, as though the staff were unsure of its reception. Anna caught several surprised looks as she hurriedly escaped, having grabbed the toy mouse. But the looks weren't directed at her. They were directed at the consultant surgeon.

CHAPTER FIVE

'Use the bloody indicator, woman. People behind you aren't telepathic, you know.'

'Don't shout at me!'

'For God's sake—get out of second gear!'

Anna wrenched the steering-wheel she was holding and jammed her foot on the brake. Not having disengaged the gear, the car gave a violent jerk and then stalled—fortunately, near the kerb. A car hooted angrily as it passed and then there was a moment's heavy silence.

'This is not a good idea, Mike.'

'I know. I'm not the patient type. Come here!' Mike's hand slid under Anna's hair and she turned her head at the gentle pressure. Her lips tried to stay unresponsive to his but it was simply not possible. It was Mike who broke the contact.

'Swap places,' he ordered.

'How am I going to learn to drive if I sit in the passenger seat?'

'We'll get further out of town so you're not quite such a menace.'

'You said I was improving.'

'Hmm. Did I?'

Anna slumped into the passenger seat. 'This was your idea, you know. Teaching me to drive.'

'How else are you going to be able to live at the beach house? It's twenty minutes away from the hospital.'

'That was your idea as well. I'm still not sure I like it. Rent-free accommodation—supplied by you. A car—supplied by you. What does that make me, I wonder?'

'A caretaker. I told you. The house and car belonged to my mother. I should have put them on the market a long time ago. Now they're too run-down to be marketable. You saw the house.'

'Only the bedroom,' Anna said wickedly. Mike had taken her to the Papamoa beach property a week ago, a day after Emily's surgery. He had deemed it the perfect answer to their logistical problem but Anna had been less than enthusiastic.

'I haven't got a car.'

'There's one with the house. It just needs a tune-up.'

'I can't drive.'

'What? Why not?'

'I've never been able to afford a car. And my father wouldn't let me learn to drive. It wasn't a woman's place.'

'How archaic.'

'You said it. I was allowed to drive the tractor. I can plough a great furrow.'

'I'll teach you to drive,' Mike had declared. 'It shouldn't be too difficult. You're moderately intelligent.'

'Gee, thanks.'

Mike's opinion seemed to have been revised on the first driving lesson. 'Perhaps your father was right. Women shouldn't drive.'

'You're very like my father. Why didn't I notice that before?'

But the acrimony had ended the instant they'd

stood together in the bedroom of the beach house. Nothing else had mattered during those hours they'd shared together at the isolated property. Apparently it had been a weekend retreat for Mike's mother many years ago. All personal effects had been removed but it had been left fully furnished and even supplied with linen and cooking utensils. Mike hadn't said how his mother had died or why he'd never used the house himself. Anna hadn't asked. She thought of it as their house, a private retreat where they could be together to share the joy of a physical relationship that only improved with familiarity.

This was the second Saturday afternoon they'd spent at the beach house and it was gone before they were aware of the time. It was Anna who suggested a walk on the beach.

'So, have you decided?'

'What about?'

'This.' Mike's wave encompassed the beach house and the small blue car parked in front of it. Anna looked at the unkempt garden, the dirty windows, the lawn that had gone to seed and covered the pathways.

'It does need somebody to look after it.'

'I told you that.'

'And it would be nice to hear the sound of the sea at night.'

'I could come out, the nights that you're not on call,' Mike told her softly. 'We could listen to the sea together.'

Anna took hold of the hand she was offered. 'OK.' She laughed. 'I'll take the position. Is there anything in the fine print I should know about?'

'Only this.' Mike tugged Anna's hand and pulled her into his arms. He smoothed the windswept strands of hair off her face and kissed her. On her forehead, her eyelids, her cheeks and finally her lips. 'I want you, Anna,' he whispered. 'I need you.'

Anna said nothing. She could have repeated the words back to him but she'd have added a third sentiment. She knew now, despite the acrimony the driving lessons had caused, that she loved Michael Smith. Loved him with a passion that frightened her. Was he making all this possible simply for ease of a physical relationship? Even if he was, wasn't it possible—no, probable—that something more would grow from it? Anna had to believe that was the case. They were travelling the same path. Surely their destination was mutual?

'I think he fancies you, Anna.'

'Who?'

'"Jaws".'

Anna's coffee-mug hit the table with a thump. She did her best to make her laugh seem natural. 'What on earth makes you say that, Ken?'

'I haven't heard him bawl you out for at least a week. In fact, he's almost less grumpy than usual when you're around.'

'Really? I must be a good influence.' Anna shrugged but made a mental note to warn Mike not to be so pleasant to her at work. She tried to change the subject. 'How's the study going, Ken?'

'Totally relentless. My social life is non-existent.' Ken was staring thoughtfully at Anna. 'You wouldn't come out with me for dinner, would you? Distract me from pre-examination nerves?'

'It's more than six months away, Ken. It's too early to be nervous but, no, sorry, I'm a bit busy. I took on this flat after I got my driver's licence and the garden needs a lot of work. It's great fun but it's taking all my spare time at the moment.'

'Oh.' Ken looked disappointed then reverted to the disconcerting subject he'd raised previously. 'I still think your boss has got his eye on you.'

'Perhaps I've just impressed him by not collapsing under the work load. I'm nearly two-thirds of the way through the run now and I think I almost know what I'm doing.'

Ken nodded. 'You're the best house surgeon we've had, that's for sure. Do you think you'll want to stay in Orthopaedics?'

'No.' Anna frowned. 'I'm not sure what I want to do yet but I'm getting a better idea of what I don't want. My next run is A and E and then it's Paediatrics. I'm really looking forward to that one. I love working with the kids.' Anna smiled, thinking of the small package in her pocket. It was a wind-up pink mouse that did somersaults. She'd found it in the hospital gift shop and it was a farewell present for Emily Jacobs, who was due for discharge today. Anna was going to miss the little girl and her mother, having become close to both of them over the last few weeks.

Ken's beeper sounded and he rinsed his coffee-mug quickly. 'I guess you're right.' He seemed unable to stay away from his preoccupation with Michael Smith. 'You're not really his type.'

'No,' Anna agreed with relief. She washed out her own mug as Ken headed for the phone. She hesitated then asked lightly, 'What *is* his type, do you think?'

Ken paused with his hand on the receiver. 'I can't imagine him having anything to do with kids. Not on a personal level. I'd say someone who's equally career-orientated.' He grinned. 'And someone tough enough to put up with his bad temper. Erica's probably right up his street. Speak of the devil,' he muttered as Erica Savage entered the ward kitchen. He turned his attention to the phone as his beeper sounded again.

'Have you got a minute, Anna? I've got two people to see in A and E. I thought you might like to come with me. It's going to be your next run, isn't it?'

'Sure.' Anna looked thoughtfully at Erica as she followed the senior registrar out of the ward. She still wouldn't say they were friends but they got on well enough in a professional setting. What did Mike think of his junior colleague? And did she even have a life away from the hospital?

'One sounds like another cervical fracture,' Erica told her as she hit the lift button. 'Car flipped and rolled and he was left hanging upside down. Apparently he thought he was OK but then found he couldn't move anything.'

'That's the second this week,' Anna said in surprise. 'I don't suppose they're all going to do as well as Tony.'

'He's been lucky,' Erica agreed. Tony's surgery had been delayed by nearly a week because of a virus that had developed into a nasty attack of bronchitis, but his progress since the operation had been astounding. He still didn't have any movement in his legs but some feeling had returned and he was optimistic. The power in his arms was now enough to enable him to play his guitar and Anna had been rapt when she'd heard the music in Room 6 for the first time a few days ago.

'We're going to transfer him to the spinal rehabilitation unit tomorrow.' Erica led the way into the emergency department. 'He should do well. He's got a good attitude.'

Anna smiled. That was high praise from Erica. She never commented on a patient's personality or how she felt about them. It was their attitude that affected her clinical relationship with them so that was all that mattered. Erica was extremely competent but her lack of warmth disconcerted Anna.

She supposed people might think of Mike as being just as coolly professional but Anna knew just how warm he could be. It was a month since she'd moved into the beach house and the amount of time they were now able to spend together hadn't diminished the eagerness they felt for each other. If anything, it was steadily increasing.

Perhaps Erica kept her passions carefully hidden from her professional colleagues as well. After Ken's comments Anna would have to tell Mike that he might not be hiding his own as well as he'd thought, however. Was their relationship really affecting him to the point of mellowing his personality? Anna rather hoped it was. She knew her own happiness had had a knock-on effect which had helped both her competence and enjoyment of her work.

Erica was in front of the X-ray viewing screens. 'Look at this, Anna. What do you think?'

Anna traced the spinal bumps beneath the outline of the skull with her fingers. 'It's a high fracture. C3, C4. Looks displaced and the spurs on the back have sheared off completely.'

'He's lucky to have made it here at all.' Erica shook her head. 'He'll need a bone graft fusion and a plate on the front. There'll be no stability at the back without those spurs. I'll get hold of Mike and see how soon we can get him into Theatre. Why don't you have a look at our other patient?'

Anna was taken to a side-room by the A and E registrar, James Hean. He'd looked pleased when Anna had introduced herself. 'We'll look forward to your next run,' he told her.

'Good idea, coming in for a taste of it now.' They stopped by the patient's bed. 'This is Lawrence Pellet. He's twenty-one—a car mechanic.'

'Hello, Lawrence. I'm Anna Kessel. I believe you'll be coming to see us in Orthopaedics next.'

The patient nodded. 'I've made a bit of a mess of my knee.'

'What happened?'

'I was working on this engine and had the radiator out. My foot slipped and my knee went into the fan. Got a bit chopped up.'

'He's not kidding,' James confirmed. 'Have a look at this.' He lifted a bloodstained section of the heavy padding over Lawrence's left knee. Anna looked at a mangled joint. Shards of the shattered patella protruded from the bleeding shreds of skin and muscle. Anna swallowed hard.

'We've given him some analgesia and a tetanus booster and started antibiotics.' James covered the wound again carefully. 'I imagine Erica will whip him into Theatre for a clean-up pretty soon but he'll need some reconstructive surgery at a later date. How's the pain now, mate?'

'I can still feel it.'

'How would you rate it on a scale of ten with one being no pain and ten being totally unbearable.'

'Five.'

'OK.' James turned to Anna. 'We're just waiting for a portable femur X-ray. We might do a femoral nerve block. Have you done one before?'

'No, never.'

'Well, watch me this time and I'll walk you through the next one when you come down here. How does that sound?'

'Fine.' Anna returned the relaxed grin. She had the feeling that she might enjoy her next run. The feeling intensified when she emerged from Lawrence's room a few minutes later to see Michael Smith in the department. It seemed they'd still have some professional contact even when she changed runs.

'We're going to put David Hayman into cervical traction until we can get him into Theatre,' Mike informed Anna. 'He's got a few other things that need checking out so we won't get to operate until tomorrow at the earliest. Erica's going to have a look at that compound patella injury so I'll get you to assist me in here, thanks.'

Anna nodded. Ken was right. Mr Smith was certainly more courteous than he used to be. She moved out of the way of another trolley coming into the resuscitation area at high speed. A and E staff moved quickly and Anna and Mike found themselves temporarily alone with their patient. A nurse had already shaved the areas of David's scalp about his ears and Anna followed Mike's instructions, painting the patches liberally with antiseptic and infiltrating the areas with local anaesthetic.

'This is just going to make sure that we don't get any accidental movement that might make your injury worse,' Mike told David. 'It's going to keep the broken bones in your neck in the right place until we can get you to Theatre and make things a bit more stable. Have we got the tongs ready, Dr Kessel?'

Anna opened the sterile packs and held the pins—still inside the packages—for Mike to grasp. A month ago she'd have been terrified of dropping one but now she felt a lot more confident. She watched as the Gardner-Wells calipers were attached on either side of David's skull.

'We just want to go far enough to grip the outer skull table,' Mike commented. 'There—that's got it. This screw's spring-loaded so we can't exceed the correct tension.'

'What weights do you want?' Anna checked the bottom of the trolley beside her.

'Five kilograms,' Mike instructed. 'And get a soft neck roll as well. We want to maintain a normal cervical curvature.'

Erica came in as Mike was making a final check of the traction set-up. 'I've sent Lawrence Pellet up to the ward. You can go and admit him, Anna. He ate a big lunch so we'll delay Theatre for a bit.'

'Mr Hayman here can go up as well,' Mike added. 'They look like they need the space in here and I'd better get going. I'm running late for my private clinic.'

Anna hoped it was an unusually busy spell for A and E as she threaded her way out through the bustle. If not, she might find it even harder to cope than she had when beginning her orthopaedics run. She was quite relieved to head back to the now familiar routines of the ward. The pressure and drama of emergencies would, no doubt, be good experience for her but while Anna felt confident she'd be able to cope she knew it wasn't an area that particularly excited her. What she was really looking forward to was the paediatric run. Anna quickened her pace. She had to make sure she had time to go and visit Emily before she left the hospital that afternoon.

With admission formalities completed on both David Hayman and Lawrence Pellet, Anna hurried to the paediatric ward. She was only just in time. Sue Jacobs had just settled Emily into her custom-built wheelchair, ready for departure. Anna dropped to a crouch beside the child and Emily wound chubby arms around her neck. Anna happily returned the enthusiastic kiss.

'I'm going to miss seeing you every day, darling. Here...' Anna fished the package out of her white coat pocket. 'I've got something for you.'

'Oh, you shouldn't have, Anna,' Sue Jacobs protested.

Anna smiled. 'Like I said, I'm going to miss you both. I'm amazed how well Emily's come through the surgery. She'll be walking before you know it.'

'I hope so. Mr Smith certainly seems confident. Will we see you at the outpatient clinics?'

Anna shook her head. 'I doubt it, Sue. I'm not even going to be on Orthopaedics much longer.'

Emily finally got through the wrapping on her gift. She held up the plastic mouse triumphantly. 'Look, Mumma! A mouse for Emmy!'

'Let me show you what it does.' Anna wound up the bright pink toy and placed it on the tray of Emily's wheelchair. With a loud squeaking noise the mouse turned repeated somersaults. Emily clapped her hands and shouted with laughter.

Sue groaned. 'It's going to drive me nuts. When

you have kids, Anna, never buy a toy that makes a noise.' But she, too, was laughing and she gave Anna a hug. 'Thanks for everything, Anna. You will come and see us at the centre, won't you?'

'I'd really like to,' Anna replied. But her tone was doubtful.

'You'll have to,' Sue said firmly. She squashed a teddy bear into an overflowing bag and held it down as she did up the zip. 'When I rang Charlotte Berry to let her know about Emily's progress I asked if it would be OK and she said she's looking forward to meeting you. You'd like her, Anna. She's an amazing woman.'

'So I've heard.' Anna felt like she already knew a lot about Chandler House, a centre for physically disabled children that many of Mike's young patients were associated with. The centre was more than a school. It catered for children from birth until the age of twelve and the staff included specialist teachers, a nurse, physiotherapists and occupational therapists. Chandler House seemed to have an aggressive-sounding approach to mobilising children and encouraging independence, but the parents of disabled children couldn't speak highly enough of the centre and even Mike had sounded impressed when Anna had asked him about it.

'Charlotte Berry is the centre's director,' he'd told her. 'She's a very determined woman. She has a vision of what can be achieved for these children and isn't about to let anything get in the way. She's accumulated amazing resources and is gaining such a reputation for results that they have quite a waiting list for admission.'

'You sound like you know her quite well.'

Mike had shrugged. 'We both deal with many of the same children. She makes it her business to involve herself with their progress on every level, including any medical intervention. She's even been here to observe surgery—like the iliopsoas transfers we've just done on Emily Jacobs.'

Yes. Anna had to admit she was intrigued by both the centre and the woman running it.

'I'll make sure I get there,' she told Sue Jacobs. 'At least that way I can find out if you're still sane after living with the gymnastic mouse.'

The late summer weather was still glorious and Anna took great delight in early morning runs on the beach and being outdoors again in the evenings. Sometimes she would keep working in the garden until well after dark, planting by a sense of touch more than anything or weeding in the pools of light near the beach-house windows. Initially, she'd launched into the relandscaping of the property from a sense of shame at being 'kept'. She had to provide more than just her physical company to someone who was providing her with both accommodation and a vehicle.

Anna had quickly fallen in love with the place, however, and her efforts took on much more scope and depth as her feelings showed. It was just as well she loved the place because more often than not she was here on her own.

Mike was frequently called in to the hospital, had weekends disrupted or returned too late from the trips to Auckland to come out to the beach house. Even with Anna's new on-call roster, which had eased the pressure considerably, they didn't manage more than two or three evenings together in a week and it was rare for Mike to stay a whole night.

Last night had been one of the exceptions and Anna had woken at dawn, her head nestled on Mike's shoulder, one arm draped across his chest. She'd propped herself up on one elbow and watched him sleeping for a while, tempted to rouse him, knowing that he'd be only too willing to continue the cycle of passion they'd been unable to break until well after midnight. Something held Anna back this time and she sighed lightly, rolling herself away from Mike's warmth and easing herself out of bed without disturbing his regular, soft breathing.

Anna slipped on an old T-shirt and shorts. It was only 6 a.m. and she had more than an hour before she needed to leave for the hospital. Going outside, Anna turned on the hose and began watering a newly planted border. Her delight in the project had become real pride when Mike had taken a tour the previous evening.

'I can't believe what you've done to the place. It looks totally different.'

'I'm not keen on straight lines in a garden. Those flower beds around the house and down each side of the path were too rigid.'

'Where's the path gone?'

'I dug it up,' Anna had admitted. 'Look—I've pegged out the new one in a nice gentle curve. I want to edge it and then fill it with a fine gravel or crushed shells. Much more in keeping with a seaside garden.'

'What the—?' Mike had stopped in his tracks.

Anna had swallowed nervously. 'You did say I could do what I liked to fix up the garden.'

'Yes…but…' Mike had been lost for words. He'd

stared at the thick hedge that bordered the garden on the beach side of the property. In the space between two tall cabbage trees that grew close to the hedge Anna had carved a large gap, creating access to the beach but leaving foliage curving over the top to form an archway.

'You need to be able to see the sea,' Anna had stated firmly. 'And look—the tree trunks frame it perfectly. Do you like the gardens underneath?'

The circular borders at the base of the cabbage trees carried on the theme Anna had used all through the new garden. Bushy white marguerite daisies were surrounded by a bright carpet of Californian poppies, nasturtiums, verbena and geraniums. Most were grown from cuttings or seeds and Anna had been thrilled with the speed with which they were filling out and starting to bloom. It was mostly due to the manure she'd added to the sandy soil and her dedication in keeping them well watered.

'I love it,' Mike replied seriously. 'You never fail to astound me, Anna Kessel. How do you know so much about gardening or is it simply another of those things you're "quite good at"?'

Anna laughed. 'Actually, I know a lot more about vegetables than flowers. My father's a market gardener. I spent a lot of my childhood tending broccoli and Brussel sprouts. My mother grew cut flowers and propagated perennials but she became too good at it so it had to stop.'

'Why?'

'My father had very clear ideas about the roles of family members. He wasn't interested in my mother running her own business. It interfered with her other duties.'

'And he wasn't keen on his daughter becoming a doctor?'

'Absolutely not. Unthinkable. I was supposed to marry a nice Dutch boy and take on my mother's role, preferably on a neighbouring market garden.'

'Surely nobody these days really believes they can control their children to that extent?'

Anna shrugged. 'Apart from me, he's succeeded rather well. My brother's taking over the farm and has married a nice Dutch girl who can cook rollmops and *zandegebak* and *speculaas* for Christmas. My mother does what's expected of her. It's a small, isolated community. People emigrated in the fifties and sixties but never assimilated. We weren't even allowed to speak English at home. I had to get out. It all comes back to expectations, I suppose, people being confined in boxes that other people create. I can't go back,' Anna added sadly. 'They wouldn't want me back, anyway. I'm too much of a threat. Boxes can be a form of security. Some people can't cope without them.'

Mike listened quietly and then drew Anna into his arms. 'You're an extraordinary woman, Anna,' he told her. 'I can understand why you want to chop holes in hedges. Even a house shouldn't be completely boxed in. Just leave some sort of a boundary. I like to know where I belong.'

Anna turned the hose off but continued to stand, staring at her garden. That was exactly what was bothering her. The boundary. Or, rather, the barrier. Their relationship seemed caught. They knew each other so well and yet they didn't know each other at all. The time they had together was wonderful but it seemed like repetitions of their first encounter. They cooked and ate together, they swam or went for walks, listened to music and made love. Only once had Anna tried a tentative push at the boundary and she'd tried to make it light-hearted.

'What is it about your home that puts it off limits for me, Mike?'

He'd looked startled. Disconcerted. 'It's not entirely my own home,' he'd said reluctantly. 'It's a bit complicated.'

Anna had smiled encouragingly. 'Are you hiding a mad aunt? Looking after a senile grandparent? Or is it being guarded by a vicious dog you can't control?'

And Mike had laughed. 'All of the above.' And he'd stifled any further queries with his lips. And his hands. She'd been easy to distract. She knew she was swimming in uncharted waters and had been more than willing to retreat to the safety of the zone they'd created.

But now the barrier was looming close again. She knew they were both aware of it but by mutual consent they were avoiding any mention of it. On Anna's part it was because she wasn't ready to push again just yet. She still hoped that their physical intimacy would somehow dissolve the obstacle. But her level of frustration was becoming increasingly difficult to dismiss. Anna felt cast in the role of a mistress. She wanted more—much more—but wasn't ready to risk losing what she already had.

It was a little like her attitude to her career. Anna knew there was something important in her life just waiting for her to be able to define it clearly. Her experience was allowing her to narrow it down by finding out what she didn't want, like a hospital career or surgery.

She was quite sure now that Michael Smith was an important part of her future. She knew it was equally as important as any career decision and her experience so far told her exactly what she didn't want. She didn't want to lose him. Her future was linked with this man but he was going to have to remove the barrier himself. Whatever it was, Anna knew it wasn't something she could remove for him. She also thought that Mike wanted to remove it.

Sometimes, when they walked on the beach together or Mike sat listening to her playing her guitar and singing and often in the few minutes of spent passion as they lay as close as physically possible, Anna felt Mike was on the verge of telling her. Of inviting her across the divide. But every time he held himself back and Anna was too frightened to encourage him.

Perhaps what she didn't know would be enough to hurt her. Enough to destroy what they both had.

CHAPTER SIX

THE child and the mother were both crying.

A nurse handed Anna the jar of jelly beans in exchange for the blood-sample vacutubes. Anna smiled. 'Thanks. Who gets one first?'

The nurse glanced at the woman sympathetically. 'I'll get Mum a cup of tea as soon as I've got these samples off.'

Anna grabbed a box of tissues as the nurse wheeled the trolley away. She pulled some out and held them against the small and very wet nose of the boy on the bed.

'Blow, Freddie,' she instructed. 'It's all over now, see?' Anna touched the tape on the boy's arm. Taking a red felt pen from her pocket, she carefully drew a smiling face onto the white strip of tape. 'Look, he's swallowed a little tube and now it's sitting inside your vein and that means we won't have to prick you with any more needles when we want to look at some blood or give you medicine.'

'Does the medicine taste bad?'

'No, it tastes like jelly beans. That's why he's got a big smile. The medicine is inside the drink he's getting from that bag.' Anna pointed to the IV fluid pack now attached to the drip. She reached for some more tissues. 'Let's wipe your face and then you can choose some jelly beans. Maybe we can give you a smiley face again. Shall we give Mum a jelly bean, too, Freddie?'

The child smiled for the first time since arriving on the ward but his mother stifled a fresh sob.

'I feel like it's all my fault.'

'It isn't,' Anna told the woman firmly as she passed her the box of tissues. 'Urinary tract infections are extremely common in children with spina bifida. Freddie's are a lot less frequent than they used to be.' Anna's note-taking on admission had been as thorough as usual. 'This is the first infection in nearly a year.'

'But this is a really bad one. They said he might have damage to his kidneys and he might need an operation. And what about his leg? I can't believe I didn't know he'd broken it.'

'Pathological fractures are also common, Judith. When they're not painful they're often not noticed unless there's a deformity or swelling. Freddie's isn't displaced so there's no deformity. Mr Smith will be in to see him soon but I don't think it's going to be a major problem. It's more important that we sort out this infection and we've made a good start on that.'

Anna eyed the IV set-up with satisfaction. It was the first time she'd put an IV line into a child and thankfully it had been achieved with minimum trauma. The staff in A and E had applied an EMLA patch when Freddie had come in, which had provided enough of a local anaesthetic to make the procedure almost painless. The tears had been more in anticipation and had quickly cleared. Anna wished Judith's distress could be so easily dealt with. She glanced at her watch. Surely it wouldn't hurt to spend a few more minutes with Freddie and his mother. She placed a small basket of toys on the bed beside Freddie.

'See what you can find in there,' she told him. 'I can see some cars and, look, what's that?'

'Dinosaur.' Freddie rummaged in the basket and Anna moved over to where Judith stood, staring out of the window.

'It must have happened last week. One of the older children pushed him over. There have been so many squabbles lately and I can't always be there to watch them.'

'It must be difficult,' Anna sympathised. Six-year-old Freddie was the third of four children. 'I suppose the others resent the extra attention Freddie needs.'

'We do our best to be fair but sometimes I'm just so tired.' Judith Higgs sighed heavily. 'That's why we went away last weekend with the other children to try and give them a special treat. But Freddie hated being with my mother and she found it all a bit much. She probably just forgot to make sure his bladder was emptying completely even though I've shown her exactly where to push on his tummy.

'I didn't even know he was running a temperature this morning. He's been difficult ever since we got back and I was so busy, getting the others off to school and having Freddie ready for his taxi. Then the nurse at Chandler House rang to say they were bringing him in here. It's Jane's birthday today. There are six children from kindergarten coming this afternoon and what am I going to do about the party? My mother can't help—she's not that well herself.'

The stress seemed to be contagious. Anna almost wished she'd left Freddie's admission to the paediatric house surgeon, but he'd been busy helping the registrar with a lumbar puncture on a child with suspected meningitis and had been delighted by Anna's offer of assistance. At least the other orthopaedic patients on the ward were straightforward cases. Anna had already checked them all before the arrival of Freddie and there was no cause for any complaints from either Michael Smith or Erica when they arrived for a brief paediatric ward round.

A five-month-old baby with a congenital dislocation of the hip was nearing the end of ten days in Gallows traction to align the joint correctly, before being fitted with a splint.

'We'll check the position on X-ray tomorrow,' Mike told the baby's mother. 'All being well, we'll be able to fit the splint and then you can take her home.'

'And if it isn't right?'

'Then we'll perform a minor operation to release the tendon and get the head of the femur in the right place. Otherwise it won't be able to develop properly. It would mean a full plaster cast instead of a splint.'

'How long for?'

'Six months.'

The mother looked dismayed. 'But how do you keep them clean?'

Mike couldn't help a quick glance at his watch. 'There's a hole cut in the plaster. The nappies go on outside.'

The mother shook her head and Anna could share her obvious misgivings. It was hard enough keeping babies clean even when the whole area was accessible.

'Don't worry,' Mike told her. 'It may not come to that but if it does you'll manage. You're a good mother.'

Anna smiled warmly at the woman as they moved

on. She certainly was a good mother and not just because she didn't go to work, which Anna suspected might be Mike's main criterion for making the judgement. She hadn't moved away from her baby's side since admission and had managed to continue breastfeeding even though it meant crawling into the cot to lie beside the immobilised baby. The technique had become increasingly difficult as the traction had progressed and the baby's legs were pulled further apart, decreasing the space that had to be negotiated under the traction ropes.

Another baby had been in for correction of a club foot the day before. Mike was happy with his condition and told his parents they could take him home. An eight-year-old boy who had needed internal fixation for a badly broken arm was also progressing well. The swelling in his fingers was receding.

'We'll keep you for another day or two, Martin,' Mike told him. 'We'll have to replace this cast when the swelling's gone right down or it'll be too loose.'

'What else have we got?' Mike's enquiry of Anna was brisk.

'I've just admitted Freddie Higgs,' Anna told him. 'He's a six-year-old boy with spina bifida and—'

'Yes, I know Freddie,' Mike interrupted. 'What's happened?'

'He appears to have a severe urinary tract infection, possibly pyelonephritis. We've taken bloods off for a white-cell count and differential, creatinine and urea for kidney function. They managed to get a midstream urine sample in A and E and I've started him on antibiotics.'

'This is all very commendable, Anna, but I didn't

think you'd started a general paediatric run yet. This is Jeff Pringle's department. Urology.'

'He's also got a fractured femur. His mother thinks it may have happened about ten days ago when he had a fall. The X-ray shows a—'

'Where's the X-ray?' Mike sounded weary and he shook his head. 'Let's hope this doesn't set Freddie back too much. He's been making such good progress.'

Mike sent Erica off to complete the discharge formalities on the baby with the club foot. Anna followed him to Freddie's room.

'Hello, Judith.'

'Mr Smith! Oh, I'm so glad you're here.'

Freddie looked as delighted as his mother at the surgeon's arrival, and Anna felt a strange surge of pride at the warmth Mike's arrival had generated. He seemed to keep such a professional detachment from his patients yet the bond was clearly there. Perhaps she wasn't alone in recognising the depth of feeling Michael Smith kept so well hidden. Even now, he seemed purely professional as he picked up Freddie's chart.

'Have we got any blood results back yet, Dr Kessel?'

'I'll go and ring,' Anna offered. 'It's an hour since we sent the bloods off.' She wished Mike could unbend just a little and call her Anna in front of patients. But at least he'd dropped the 'Van'.

'Give Urology a call as well. I want to know what's going on with Freddie's kidney function as soon as possible.'

The results still weren't available but Mike didn't appear too annoyed. 'Did you get hold of Urology?'

'The registrar's on his way.'

'Good. He can sort that one out.' Mike was holding an X-ray plate up to the window. 'Here's the fracture, Judith. It's actually started to heal by itself—that's the callus formation you can see around the fracture line. Fortunately it's in a good position, which is good news in that we won't have to immobilise Freddie. We'll get on top of this kidney infection and have him back on his feet in a day or two. Charlotte tells me he's doing extremely well at school.'

Judith nodded. 'He loves it.' Then she frowned. 'It was Charlotte who brought Freddie in this morning and waited until I could get here. She was very worried. I'd better ring her.'

'I'll be talking to her later,' Mike said. 'I'll let her know what's happening.'

Anna was surprised by Mike's casual response. He sounded as though contact with the director of Chandler House was a daily occurrence. Anna was reminded of her promise to Sue Jacobs to visit Emily's school. Thanks to her last weekend on call, the new roster gave her a weekday off this week. It could be the ideal opportunity to visit Chandler House. Her curiosity was further piqued by Mike's reference to Charlotte Berry. Anna's thoughts were interrupted when Mike's beeper sounded.

'That's Theatre,' he announced, checking the number. 'They'll have David Hayman ready.' He glanced at Anna. 'You wanted to observe this neck fusion surgery, didn't you?'

Anna had to walk fast to keep pace with Mike. 'Judith Higgs is really stressed,' she informed the consultant. 'It must be very difficult to cope with a large family, including a disabled child. Did you know they've never even been away on holiday since Freddie was born? They try one weekend and now Judith feels it was a disaster because Freddie's sick. It's pretty rough if they can never get a break.'

'There's help available.'

'Chandler House isn't residential at all, is it? Even short term?'

'No. Children should be with their families,' Mike stated. 'Particularly disabled children.'

'Of course.' Anna passed through the door to the stairwell, which Mike held open for her. 'But you can't expect whole families to cope with that sort of stress without a break now and then.'

'Responsibilities mean sacrifice. A disabled child suffers enough, without being institutionalised even short term. Or put into foster-care, no matter now good it might be.'

'The disabled child isn't the only victim.' Anna couldn't believe Mike's views were so rigid. 'The whole family suffers. It's not a case of a clear-cut set of duties to be adhered to no matter what. How would you feel if you were Freddie's father? If you had a wife and three other children towards whom you had responsibilities?'

Mike stopped suddenly, his hand on the stair rail. Anna nearly bumped into him.

'I will never be in that position.'

Anna stepped down so that she was two steps below the consultant. She had to look a long way up to meet Mike's eyes. The spark of anger she saw instantly ignited her own feelings of indignation. 'Do you have some sort of divine protection? You can guarantee you'll never have a disabled child?'

'Yes.'

'How?'

'Because I don't intend having *any* children.'

Anna moved closer to the stair rail as two harassed-looking junior doctors went past, taking the stairs two at a time. She felt a wave of shock. Was this it? Had she finally come up against the barrier? Her voice was a whisper. 'You mean you don't want to have any children? Or you can't?'

'Does it matter? The result is the same. We were discussing a patient, Anna. This isn't about me. Why make it personal?' Mike's beeper sounded but he didn't move.

'Because it *is* personal,' Anna said heatedly. 'You have such black and white expectations of people. Of what they should and shouldn't be doing. What gives you the right to make these judgements?'

'Everybody makes their own judgements according to their own moral code. Whether I approve or disapprove of how people live their lives makes no difference to how I treat them.' His voice was cold. 'I hope you're not suggesting that my opinions influence my professional responsibilities?'

'No, of course not. That's why it's a personal issue.' Anna's neck was beginning to feel strained as she stared up at Mike. 'What about people who want to share more than a professional relationship with you? Perhaps you should fill me in on your expectations in that area. You don't intend having children. Do you intend having a wife? Just where do I fit in, Mike?'

Mike finally moved. He stepped down twice to stand beside Anna, his arm resting on her stomach as he continued to hold the stair rail. 'Where you are right now,' he said quietly.

A hum of voices and clatter of footsteps announced a group of people on their way up the staircase. Mike dropped his arm and kept his voice low. 'I don't want to be without you, Anna. I want you to be happy with what I am able to give you. Isn't that enough?'

At the curious glances the group of nurses cast in their direction Mike turned. He only just caught Anna's reply as he began to move up the stairs again.

'No,' Anna said sadly. 'I don't think it is enough.'

She'd rattled him, Anna could tell. Nobody else could, of course, but Anna knew it was the reason Mike had invited her to assist with the surgery instead of just observing. Erica had seemed unsurprised but, then, her level of professional detachment was almost as well developed as that of Mike. In any event, the operation was a complex procedure and perhaps an extra pair of hands was a welcome addition.

'We'll use a modified Southwick, Smith-Robinson approach,' Mike announced when the anaesthestist had intubated and induced David. 'Let's get him packed and stretched.'

Anna stood back as the nursing team swung into action. A small pack was placed between David's shoulder blades, a rolled towel went under his neck to support it and his head was placed on a doughnut-shaped piece of foam rubber. The head was turned to the right after Mike had marked a line just under David's chin with a felt pen. He drew another line on the patient's hip.

'You can get the graft out for us, Erica.' Mike turned to the anaesthetist. 'Let's have six kilograms of head-halter traction.'

The anaesthetist nodded. With the Gardner-Wells

calipers already attached to David's skull, it was simply a matter of adjusting the weights. Two nurses attended to the tape attached to the foot of the table, positioning it around David's shoulders to apply a counter-traction, and Anna could understand Mike's earlier instruction. David Hayman looked both well packed and stretched.

Mike wasted no time. His initial incision and dissection was rapid and confident. Anna was kept busy ligating blood vessels.

'Get ready with a retractor, Anna. We'll retract the oesophagus and trachea towards the midline and the carotid sheath laterally.'

Anna was concentrating too hard to notice Mike's use of her given name. Beside her, Erica was leaning against a brace and bit, slowing turning the handle as she removed a cylindrical piece of bone from David's hip. Anna handed Mike another brace and bit at his request.

'This one's smaller than the one Erica's using,' Mike commented. 'That way the graft is slightly oversized so it'll be a good, tight fit.' He positioned the instrument against the disc between the third and fourth vertebrae. 'The diameter of the cervical vertebra is 1.7 centimetres,' he told Anna. 'This is calibrated to go to 2 but we don't want to go that far because we'd be into the spinal cord.' He turned the handle carefully, his attention on the calibration markings.

Erica asked for a screwdriver, which the theatre nurse supplied. She tapped out the plug of bone she'd removed into a kidney dish and handed it to Anna. 'There's a spike on the end of the punch,' Erica instructed. 'Load the bone graft onto that.'

Anna took the piece of bone gingerly in her gloved hand. She could feel a trickle of perspiration run down her back but didn't dare even contemplate the thought of dropping anything. The stress was unbearable and wasn't relieved even when the punch, safely holding the bone graft, was in position and Mike was hammering the graft into place. Anna knew at that point that, fascinating as it was, a career as a surgeon was definitely not for her. She could only admire the calm confidence of the team around her as the long procedure continued.

A titanium plate was fitted over the graft. Mike drilled the holes but Anna was allowed to tighten the tiny screws. One went on each corner, the two top screws into the third vertebra and the two bottom ones held the fourth. A fifth central screw went directly into the bone graft. Anna's nerves were stretched to breaking point as she tightened the final screw and stood back to let Mike check her work.

'Well done. We'll make a surgeon of you yet.'

Anna was still too tense to recognise the first professional compliment Michael Smith had paid her. It took some time to close up but it wasn't until David had been released from traction and fitted into a moulded collar to support his neck that Anna realised how exhausted she was. A glance at the clock astonished her. They'd been in Theatre for nearly four hours. She followed Erica towards the showers gratefully. Anna was on call tonight and needed serious refreshing at the mere thought.

There were no overnight admissions serious enough to call in a consultant and Mike was away in Auckland the next day at his regular private clinic in that city. Anna wondered whether he'd make the effort to contact her when he returned or even come out for the night. Had what she'd said made him think about their relationship and where they might be headed? But she heard nothing and the following day was her day off. She worked in the garden all morning but at lunchtime, after a quick phone call, she changed into clean jeans and a sweatshirt and headed into town. She thoroughly enjoyed the drive. Her confidence had increased to the point where she couldn't believe she'd ever done without the freedom that the ability to drive—and a vehicle—had given her.

Her visit to Chandler House was a wonderful experience. Charlotte Berry was welcoming and only too pleased to show her around.

'I've heard about you,' she told Anna with a charming smile. 'You have wonderful musical abilities.'

Anna was astonished. Had Mike been talking about her in one of his conversations with Charlotte? What could he have said and why would he even be discussing her? Anna looked more closely at the woman walking beside her. Charlotte Berry was probably in her late thirties, elegantly dressed, beautifully made up and had an air of confidence about who she was and what she was doing which Anna immediately envied. She felt young, inexperienced and scruffy beside her companion. Charlotte was obviously a career woman, devoted to the path she'd chosen.

Anna could see why Chandler House had such an amazing reputation. The resources were astounding, the staff as dedicated as their director and the children enthusiastic and happy in their varied activities. The buildings were all purpose-built and well kept. Even the grounds were immaculately groomed, with a profusion of colour in the garden borders. Most people seemed to credit Charlotte Berry with single-handedly achieving such a superior establishment.

'Most places under government funding are struggling to provide adequate services these days,' Anna commented. 'How do you manage to do so well?'

'We have an active fund-raising committee,' Charlotte replied. 'I keep up contacts with business sponsors and we're lucky enough to have some generous private patrons. It's hard work but well worth while, I'm sure you agree.'

'Absolutely. And I'm not surprised about your waiting list for admissions here.'

When Anna was taken into a junior classroom she was delighted to see Emily Jacobs, still in her double hip spica plaster. The toddler was in a low trolley, crowing with delight as she was pushed around by an older child who was wearing long calipers and managing to manipulate both the crutches and the trolley at an alarming speed. Two children in the room were in wheelchairs, three others had varying degrees of supportive ironwork but all seemed to be mobile. The two teachers and their aide called the class to some sort of order to greet their visitors. Emily held up her arms to Anna who picked her up out of the trolley.

'Mouse broke,' Emily told her. 'I cried.'

'Never mind,' Anna said. 'I know where those mice come from. I'll ask Mummy if she can stand having another one in the house.'

'You know Emily, of course.' Charlotte smiled. 'And probably some of the others.'

'Hello, Todd.' Anna waved at the boy, pleased to

see him moving again so well after his foot surgery. 'I don't suppose Freddie's back at school yet.'

'Soon, I hope,' Charlotte responded. 'Mike tells me he's going home today. Most of these children are under his care,' she continued. 'Some have been all their lives and he's played a major part in getting them walking. He's a part of the family around here.'

Anna hugged Emily again and put her back into her trolley. No wonder Mike had sounded casual about his association with Chandler House, but why had he never really talked to her about it? It had to be a significant part of his life and Anna felt excluded. Did he think she wouldn't be interested? If so, he was very wrong. Anna loved the environment. When Charlotte was called to a meeting Anna begged to be allowed to stay in the classroom for a while longer.

When the director returned some time later she found Anna cross-legged on the floor of the classroom, a guitar on her lap, singing for the children. The neighbouring senior class had joined them and the room was packed. The song was causing great hilarity and Anna was trying to teach the children the tongue-twisting words to a nonsense song. Even the teachers were having trouble with the chorus about the proper cup of coffee from the copper coffee-pot.

Charlotte smiled at Anna with real warmth as she walked back with her towards the car park afterwards. 'I have another meeting, I'm afraid, but please come again. The children had told me about your musical gift and it's one area we don't get enough of.' She looked keenly at Anna. 'You have a wonderful rapport with these children. Have you considered taking your career in this sort of direction?'

'I am now,' Anna answered seriously. 'I love being

with them and I'd rather see them enjoying themselves than suffering painful treatments or illness.'

'It's not all fun here,' Charlotte responded swiftly.
'These children have to work very hard. We want
them to achieve their full potential.'

'A bit of fun can't hurt, though.' Anna turned for
a final wave towards the windows of the classroom.
'I'd love to come again.' She felt relieved to find
Charlotte's knowledge of her musical talent hadn't
come from Mike. Perhaps their relationship was
purely professional, the link only through the children
whose welfare they had in common. But for some
reason she couldn't dismiss the errant thought that
Ken would consider Miss Charlotte Berry exactly the
type of woman 'Jaws' might be interested in. Anna
tried to change the direction of her thoughts.

'The gardens are beautiful. You must have quite a
team of gardeners.'

Charlotte laughed. 'No, only Nicholas. He used to
be a pupil here but now we employ him as grounds-
man. He's passionate about plants. He also gets on
extremely well with the younger children and is a
good example of someone succeeding with quite a
severe disability. That's Nicholas over there.'

Anna followed Charlotte's gaze and saw a lanky
young man, pushing a wheelbarrow. He appeared to
have cerebral palsy and his movements were awkward enough to endanger the load in the barrow with
each uneven step.

'I must go,' Charlotte apologised. 'I have an important appointment.'

On impulse, Anna took a few minutes to wander
through the gardens, before returning to her car. She
was so impressed that she followed another impulse

and walked over to where the wheelbarrow was parked.

'You must be Nicholas,' she said, smiling.

His curly brown head jerked back and his facial muscles struggled but no intelligible sound emerged. The lad's face reddened but Anna smiled warmly and touched his shoulder.

'I'm Anna,' she told him. 'I love flowers and I think you're doing a fantastic job.'

Nicholas was still unable to respond and appeared to be very agitated by her approach so Anna just smiled again and gave him a casual wave. 'See you again, Nicholas.'

Nearing her car, Anna turned to look at Chandler House once more. She had a feeling that she'd found something of great significance. Maybe this was the direction her career should take. But to forget all the years of hardship and training and give up medicine? It was a big step. Her attention was diverted by a familiar car that cruised into the car park beside her.

'Mike! What are you doing here?' Anna felt awkward. Their last personal contact had been tense and she had the distinct feeling that he wasn't pleased to see her now.

'I could ask you the same thing, Anna.'

'It's my day off. I've been wanting to visit Chandler House ever since Sue Jacobs told me how wonderful it is. I have to agree. It's an amazing place and Charlotte Berry is an impressive woman.'

'Mmm.' Mike was offhand. Now Anna was sure he wasn't happy. Was it because she was in an unexpected setting? Or was he simply not happy to see her at all? Anna tried to sound equally offhand.

'So, what's your excuse, then?'

'Sorry?'

'For being here.' Anna was beginning to feel distinctly uncomfortable.

'My private rooms are just across the road. I thought you knew that.'

'Mmm.' It still wasn't an explanation. Mike pointed a remote control at his car and the alarm chirruped in response.

'I have to go, Anna. I've got an appointment. I'll see you later.'

'At the beach house?'

'Of course.'

Anna felt dismissed. Mike had an appointment. Charlotte Berry had an *important* appointment. It wasn't hard to put two and two together. She drove away, feeling disturbed. She'd told Mike that what he was giving her wasn't enough. Was he unable to give her more because of other commitments? Anna wished she had the courage to confront her fears. Maybe if she bought something nice for dinner and a good bottle of wine they might be able to talk about it tonight. It was certainly worth trying but she'd have to hurry to get some cash from the bank to go shopping with.

A few minutes later Anna found herself staring in consternation at the slip of paper telling her the balance in her bank account. 'There must be some mistake here,' she informed the bank teller. 'A rather serious one.'

The teller looked anxious. 'You'd better speak to the manager.'

The manager's expression of sympathetic concern relaxed into amusement as Anna explained the problem. 'Having too much money in one's account is an unusual complaint, Dr Kessel.'

'But it shouldn't be there,' Anna insisted. 'The majority of my salary goes in automatic payment for debt servicing. There must have been a mix-up.' The thought of the extra interest accruing was alarming.

'Let's have a look.' The manager turned to the computer on his desk and began tapping in Anna's account number. Suddenly his smile broadened. '*Van* Kessel. Of course, I dealt with this myself. Your debt has been cleared, Doctor. The full amount of your salary will now automatically go into your cheque account. Unless you'd like to open a savings account as well?'

Anna shook her head. 'I don't understand.' But she had a horrible feeling that she understood only too well. 'I'd like to know who made this arrangement, please.'

It seemed a long wait before Mike arrived at the beach house that evening. Anna knew he'd have gone from Chandler House back to the hospital to check on his in-patients. Or perhaps he hadn't. Perhaps his discussion with Charlotte Berry had been too enjoyable to curtail. Anna had finally reached the end of her tether. She might have been too wary to push at the boundaries of their relationship before but now she was too furious not to. When the black BMW pulled up beside the beach house Anna wasted no time. Mike seemed astonished at her angry outburst.

'I thought you'd be happy about it,' he defended himself. 'I don't understand why you're so upset.'

'I wasn't thrilled about being your ''holiday fling''.' Anna tried to keep her voice calm. 'If you remember, I also wasn't thrilled about the idea of living here as a "kept woman".'

'Don't be ridiculous,' Mike snapped. 'You make it sound like your sexual favours are all that I'm interested in.'

'That's what it feels like,' Anna shouted. 'I'm living here in *your* house. I'm driving *your* car.'

'My mother's house. My mother's car.'

Anna ignored him. 'Now I find you've deposited thousands—no, tens of thousands—of dollars into my bank account. I feel like a...a...*prostitute*!'

'For God's sake, Anna.' Mike was angry now. Very angry. 'You said I wasn't giving you enough. I thought it was what you wanted.'

Anna was disgusted. 'I wasn't talking about your *money*!'

'What were you talking about?'

'You. Us. I want more of *you*, Mike. Not just your time as a lover. And certainly not your money.' Anna couldn't stop the tears that suddenly escaped or the words she hadn't intended to say. 'I love you, Mike. I want to share your life.'

There was a moment's silence. Mike reached out to grasp Anna's shoulders. 'You do share my life,' he said, his voice catching. 'A very important part of it.'

'Exactly!' Anna broke away from his grasp. 'A *part* of it. Nobody at work is allowed to know about us. I get two or three evenings with you a week. You've never told me where you go or what you do when you're not with me. You wouldn't even tell me why you were at Chandler House today or what your relationship with Charlotte Berry is. I've never even seen where you live, for God's sake.'

'I told you right at the beginning that I didn't think

I could offer you what you wanted in a relationship, Anna. I thought you accepted that.'

'How do you know what I want? Do you assume I want marriage? A career? Children that you can't, or won't, have? A claim on a hundred per cent of your time? Have you ever asked me what I want?' Anna turned away from Mike and began to pace across the room. 'What do *you* want, Mike?'

'I want to be with you. As much as possible. I need you, Anna. It may not be perfect but it's the best I've ever found. Or ever will.'

'What's to stop us making it perfect, Mike?' Anna felt so tense her whole body was aching. 'What is it that you *really* want?'

The silence was unnerving. Anna watched as Mike finally broke the intense gaze they were sharing and slowly sat down at the table.

'You tell me my expectations of people are too rigid. That I need to compromise. To make allowances for individual situations. Why can't you make allowances for me?'

'Why can't you tell me why I need to make allowances?' Anna shot back. 'Instead of trying to buy me off?'

'It's only money, Anna,' Mike said wearily. 'What else have I got to give you?'

Anna pulled out a chair at the other end of the table. She sat down, feeling suddenly drained. The anger had gone. 'A relationship, Mike,' she said quietly. 'A real relationship—without invisible barriers. I want to be with you. I want to give you everything I have to give.' Anna sighed.

'You won't let me do that. You're boxing me in. I don't expect perfection, Mike, but you have to want something to be the best it can possibly be. Otherwise there's no point in trying. You can't set rules and refuse to break them no matter what. You have to follow your instincts. Chase your dreams. Even if they don't always turn out the way you want them to.'

'Maybe this is the best it can be.' The tawny eyes were like dark pools. Even the golden tints were hidden.

'Maybe it is,' agreed Anna. 'And maybe that would be good enough. But I can't know that because you won't let me share enough of your life to be able to judge. I cross bridges when I get to them, Mike. Life is full of unknowns and if you never try a new direction you're not going to go anywhere. You don't cross bridges. You put up gates in front of them. And then you lock the gates.'

'What are you trying to tell me, Anna?'

'That our relationship is too important to me to be allowed to get boxed in and die. I'd hoped that you'd come to feel the same way but your actions at the bank show that you don't feel the same way at all. I don't want to share your money, Mike. I want to share your life. All of it.' Anna swallowed hard. 'Or none of it. Halfway isn't good enough.'

Mike stared at her. She could see the tension in his face. 'Don't do this, Anna. Don't push me.'

'You've pushed me, Mike. Right up against one of your precious boundaries.'

Mike stood up. 'I think I'd better go. Give you some time to calm down and think about things.'

'I've had more than enough time to think.' Anna also stood up. 'I'll be going to the bank tomorrow. I'll arrange a new loan and repay your money.'

'I don't want it.' Mike was walking towards the door. 'I have no more interest in my money than you apparently have.' His voice was chilling. 'Consider it compensation for the amount of your time I've taken up. Not to mention the effort and expense you've had in relandscaping this property.'

'Payment for services rendered,' Anna said bitterly. 'And landscaping wasn't the only service provided, was it, Mike?' She raised her voice so that Mike could hear her behind the door he'd just closed.

'I hope it was worth it!'

CHAPTER SEVEN

THE envelope was still sitting on Mike's desk nearly a month later.

It contained keys. Keys to the beach house and keys for the car. Anna had left the envelope with his secretary the day she'd moved out of the beach house and now it sat, a symbol of everything he'd lost.

Why couldn't Anna have accepted what they had. It had been good. So very good. And he'd tried so hard to make it right again. He'd sent her flowers. No, he hadn't sent them—he'd carried the huge bouquet into the hospital himself. A neon sign, advertising their relationship. Mike knew many of the staff were still talking about it. He also knew that the assumption was that it had been a farewell gesture to mark the end of Dr Kessell's run in Orthopaedics, however aberrant the behaviour had been on his part.

He'd even persuaded Anna to meet him. A private meeting but still on hospital grounds. He'd told her the truth. Part of it, anyway. He'd told her that he loved her. She hadn't doubted his sincerity. That much was obvious by how upset she'd been. But it hadn't been enough. Mike could remember every broken word she'd said to him.

'You have all these neat little boxes that people are supposed to fit into, Mike. Career women are fine but not if they have children. Mothers are great but not if they work. Doctors have to be so professional at all times. A lover is acceptable but only if she stays in her assigned box.' The tears had flowed over her pale cheeks and it had been all Mike could do not to draw her into his arms, to smooth away the dampness with his lips. Anna must have sensed his desire. She'd drawn away.

'People won't be put in boxes, Mike. I was brought up in a box. I spent years fighting to get out of it. What's more important in life? A set of rules or relationships with other people? Sometimes the rules have to be bent—the edges of the boxes blurred. It's called compromise. Perhaps it's not something you're capable of.'

But what if he'd told her the truth? All of it? It would have been Tricia all over again, only much worse. Coping with disabled people on a professional basis—that was one thing. Having close contact for a major part of a personal life—that was something quite different. Mike had divided his life rigidly, he knew that. But he'd done it for protection. His own, his brother's and, more recently, to protect the relationship he had with Anna Kessel.

He'd known the protective barriers wouldn't last for ever. He had, in fact, desperately hoped they might be able to be removed. He'd been tempted to try on many occasions but the possible consequences had been too much to risk just yet. And Anna hadn't given him enough time.

And yet Anna already knew Nicholas. Her shift work in A and E gave her weekdays off more often than weekends and it seemed she spent all her free time at Chandler House. Nicholas adored her.

It had taken Mike years to win the trust and love of the brother who'd been abandoned to foster-care at birth and whom Mike hadn't even met until he'd been at medical school. It had been more years until Mike had made the commitment to care for his brother, to find the home and housekeeper suitable to make the commitment possible. Tricia had been the final catalyst. It had been then that Mike had taken Nicholas to live with him, had made the choice to live and work in a smaller centre than his ambitions were happy with. Had given up the idea that a wife and children were part of his own future.

But Anna had won his brother's heart instantly. And Nicholas had confessed to Mike how hard he tried to be with the young doctor. He picked flowers for her from the gardens at Chandler House and had begun to sneak into the classrooms whenever Anna picked up a guitar. Now it seemed they spent time together every day she visited. He was mulching all the gardens on Anna's advice, using organic sprays on the roses and redesigning a set of pathways to follow curves instead of straight lines.

He knew nothing of Mike's relationship with Anna, and Anna had no idea that Nicholas was his brother. There was really no reason not to tell her now. Except that the knowledge might make her friendship with Nicholas change and Mike didn't want his brother hurt. He trusted so few people.

Mike had tried to make him understand that Anna would eventually move on. She might even tire of her interest in Chandler House before her house-surgeon position in the city finished. But he didn't want to jeopardise that interest while it lasted. Mike had never seen Nicholas so happy. It twisted the knife in his own heart a little deeper every day.

There must be some way he could change things. Anna had been right. Their relationship was too im-

portant to allow it to die. There must be something
he could give her—a symbol of compromise or a re-
minder of what they'd had together. The idea of pre-
senting her with a gift-wrapped red Porsche was appealing but he knew that would go down like a lead
balloon. Anna had followed through her promise to
renegotiate a loan and repay the money he'd deposited in her account.

Mike suddenly realised how late he was for his
ward round. It was 8 a.m. already. The juniors would
think he was going soft. But perhaps he needed to
soften up. The house surgeon who'd replaced Anna
on the orthopaedic run had fled in tears on her first
day. She was a competent young woman, too. An
embryonic Erica Savage—well groomed and confident of her abilities and career choice. Far more so
than Anna Kessell had been to start with.

But it had been only too easy to cut her down to
size. His resentment of her for taking Anna's place
had fuelled his negative approach. Michael Smith's
reputation for being temperamental and impossible to
please had consolidated considerably in the last
month. And, right now, he really didn't care. There
was too much else to feel miserable about.

Eight a.m. Anna had done a night shift in A and E
and was due to finish for the day. She was getting
used to the full-on workload of daytime shifts in the
emergency department but the night had been relatively quiet. Almost boring. Anna had been more than
ready to deal with the young patient who'd arrived
half an hour previously. Blake Rennie was ten years
old and part of a junior swimming squad for a local
club. Arriving late for his training session, the boy

had run around the side of the pool, slipped on the wet tiles and fallen heavily onto his side.

'I heard a big click and my leg hurt,' he told the house surgeon on arrival.

Anna wasn't surprised his leg had hurt. The big click had been the ball on the head of his femur shearing off where it met the hip socket.

'The ambulance came and they gave me this gas stuff to breathe and they put this thing on my leg. It hurt heaps.'

The Hare traction splint with the pole frame and the Velcro-fastened webbing straps was still in place. The ratchet wheel attached to the webbing, which went in a figure eight around Blake's foot, had been tightened until the initial pain intensity had been decreased. Anna slipped a finger under the webbing around Blake's thigh once more. Any internal bleeding could be causing swelling that might make the fastening tight enough to compromise his circulation. She checked the pulses in his feet again as well, then looked up as Ken Slater entered the cubicle.

'Hi, there!' Anna was pleased to see the orthopaedic registrar. 'Long time, no see.'

'We're missing you upstairs, Anna. How's it going?'

'I haven't dropped anything vital yet.' Anna smiled. 'This is Blake Rennie. I told you about him on the phone. Have you seen his X-rays?'

Ken nodded. 'Hi, Blake. I'm Dr Slater. We're going to put you off to sleep for a while and fix up this broken leg for you.' He turned to Anna. 'When did he last eat?'

'He missed breakfast,' Anna told him. 'He was running late for training so he hasn't eaten anything since last night.'

'Good. We've got a theatre free at the moment. Would you like to come up and help?'

'Uh…' Anna hesitated. She'd like to watch the procedure and was now off duty officially but the possibility of running into Mike was off-putting. 'Who's doing it?'

'Me.' Ken grinned as though he guessed at the reason for Anna's reluctance. 'Tim McPherson's doing a hip replacement next door so he'll come in when he's finished.'

Anna hoped her relief didn't show. She'd barely seen Mike since starting in A and E. Orthopaedic consults were generally dealt with by the registrars and if injuries were serious enough to call in the consultant surgeon then Anna was usually too busy dealing with other aspects of the case to have much contact. It made casual meetings so much more difficult to handle, however, especially since the day Mike had told her he loved her.

Even knowing that Anna couldn't return to their previous relationship, however hard it was to resist. She'd said she wanted all or nothing and Mike hadn't offered to change the ground rules. Anna's determination, having decided on a course to take, was something well practised. She hadn't returned to the beach house since the morning after their fight about the money. Anna had packed her bags and taken a taxi into the hospital, leaving the keys to both the house and the borrowed car with Mike's secretary.

She missed the house terribly. Her room in the house-surgeons' quarters was miserably confining after that freedom. There was no early morning run on the beautiful stretch of beach, no being lulled to sleep by the gentle rumble of distant surf. She missed the garden even more. Was anybody watering the borders and had that hedge of lavender filled out enough for a first trim? But she wouldn't go back to look. She wouldn't even return for her guitar, which had been forgotten in the emotional departure. She missed her music as well as everything else but the feelings of loss paled in comparison to how much she was missing Mike. Anna felt horribly lonely.

That was partly why she was so pleased to see Ken and why she was keen to avoid her own company for a while longer and accompany Blake Rennie to Theatre. It gave her quite a jolt, standing at the doors of the scrub room and looking through the small, square window at the gowned and masked figures in the operating room. Any one of them could have been Mike. Anna sighed heavily as she pushed the door open with her shoulder.

Her fear at pushing at the bounderies of their relationship and losing what she had already had been justified. The result had been exactly what she hadn't wanted. But how could she back down now? Anna doubted that she would even be offered the opportunity to back down. She had a distinct feeling that Michael Smith could be just as stubborn on a point of principle as she was.

Tim McPherson had finished his hip replacement and was delighted to see Anna. She was struck by the relaxed atmosphere in the theatre. Staff were chatting and laughter frequent. Anna doubted that Tim McPherson had ever been as intense in his work as Michael Smith.

'Come and have a look here, Anna. Ken can get the ball rolling—so to speak.'

There was more laughter and Anna responded to the consultant's gesture and moved towards him. He pointed out a section of the illuminated set of X-rays.

'The break has dislodged the growth plate, see? It could cause a deformity or retard growth completely if we don't get it just right. We'll need to pin it.'

Ken was holding Blake's leg under the knee with one arm, twisting his ankle with his other hand, stretching and lifting the leg at the same time. An X-ray machine was linked to an image-enhancer on the wall and they all watched until the alignment of the bones was pronounced satisfactory. A theatre nurse moved in at that point, painting the leg with antiseptic. Another unrolled a plastic sheet that hung from a frame above the side of the table. The sheet was like a flexible window, part of which adhered to the operating site, providing a sterile field through which the surgeon could work.

Tim and Anna watched the image enhancer as Ken drilled a hole through a tiny incision on Blake's thigh. Two holes were made and Ken inserted guide-wires, before asking Anna to slip the hollow screws over the wires. Tim McPherson nodded his approval as Ken and Anna finished tightening the screws and then removed the guide-wires.

'That should hold things just fine.'

'How long will he need the pins for?' Anna enquired.

'He's got a few more years of growth yet. We'll probably leave them in until then. We'll keep him in for a day or two just now. Are you on Paediatrics yet, Anna?'

'No. Still A and E.'

'That'll be keeping you busy.'

'It's not too bad.' Anna stripped off her mask and gloves. 'It feels quite civilised with such definite shifts and time off during the day so often.'

The time off before afternoon shifts and whole days off after several days on were saving Anna's sanity to a large degree. She was able to escape the hospital environment and do what she chose. Her choice led, more and more often, to visiting Chandler House. They all welcomed her. In fact, they seemed to expect her now. She was an honorary staff member, loved by the children—especially for the music she provided—and appreciated by the staff for the enthusiastic encouragement she gave the children in other endeavours.

But Anna didn't spend all her time in the classrooms. She was often seen spending time talking to the parents of the children or making a contribution to the upkeep of the grounds in the company of Nicholas. It all helped fill the huge void in her life that leaving the beach house—and Mike—had created. The process had been gradual but Anna now depended on the contact with the centre for her own well-being. Having caught up on a few hours' sleep after assisting with Blake Rennie's surgery, Anna once again set off on the familiar route to Chandler House.

It was a gorgeous day. No wonder Tauranga had such a reputation for its good weather. It was a very popular city to retire to and also attracted hordes of holidaymakers. Anna was reluctant to go inside straight away and walked around the gardens of Chandler House to enjoy the warmth of the afternoon a little longer. A few minutes later she saw the awkward progress of Nicholas approaching her. He carried a bunch of flowers.

'Oh—Friesias. My favourite!' Anna exclaimed, burying her nose into the fragrant, bright yellow roses. 'And no aphids! Did you try the garlic or the rhubarb spray, Nicky?'

'Gar... Gar...' His contorted expression became frustrated.

'Garlic.' Anna nodded as though the word had been completed. Nicholas grinned and wagged his head in agreement. To a casual observer his attempt at nodding would have implied a negative response but Anna knew him well enough now. 'Did you know you can plant the cloves around the base of the bushes?' Anna asked. 'It's supposed to work just as well but I've never tried it. How's the new path coming along?'

Nicholas made an enthusiastic sound and caught Anna's hand.

'Okay, I'm coming. Don't pull my arm off!'

Nicholas laughed. It was almost like a seal barking, Anna thought, but she found it as contagious as little Emily Jacobs's giggles. It was easy to make Nicholas laugh, especially now that he was used to her. Anna remembered her second visit to Chandler House. It had been a week or so after her break-up with Mike and she'd been feeling terrible. Time with the children and a few songs had lifted her spirits and she'd been amused to see Nicholas trying to weed a garden outside the classroom window at the same time as watching what was happening inside. Then, as she was leaving, he'd come up to her in the car park, a bunch of flowers in his hand.

Anna had accepted the flowers with real pleasure but had been concerned at the obvious distress the boy had been experiencing in trying to talk to her. She'd caught one of his jerking hands and held it tightly.

'It's OK, Nicholas,' she'd said gently. 'I know the words are all in there and I know it's hard to get them out. You can say a lot without talking at all, you know. And I like what you've said with these lovely flowers.'

That had been weeks ago now and at times Nicholas relaxed enough to make a conversation relatively easy. Sometimes Anna worked in the garden with him and that was the best time for talking. When he was concentrating on something else it made Nicholas forget how awkward he was, and occasionally he managed a long sentence without a pause. Anna was impressed with the boy's knowledge of plants and even more impressed by his determination to succeed as independently as possible. If he was a typical result of education at Chandler House then he was the best advertisement the school could have.

After a tour of the grounds with Nicholas, Anna's plan to enter the classroom was again forestalled. Walking past the main office building, she found Judith Higgs sitting on a bench that was built around the trunk of an old tree. The young mother was crying. Anna sat down beside Judith and listened to a tale of woe. Freddie had developed pressure sores from his calipers, Jane had suddenly refused to eat anything, the older children were constantly squabbling and the cat had been run over. Anna shook her head and Judith finally managed a watery smile.

'Thanks, Anna. I feel better now. It all seems a bit

much now and then and I need to get it all off my chest. My husband, John, gets sick of hearing it all so often so I try not to complain too much. But now Freddie's got this new setback and he can't even wear his calipers, let alone go for his mobility assessment next week. He's really upset about it. He was going to get a prize when he reached his next goal. The other mothers here seem to cope so much better than I do. What's wrong with me, Anna?'

'Nothing.' Anna smiled. 'And I'll bet the other mothers have just as many problems. Do you go to the support group meetings?'

'I can't.' Judith sighed. 'There's always too much to do and John works long hours. Babysitters aren't that keen to come to my place.'

'You need a break, Judith,' Anna told her thoughtfully. 'A real holiday. Freddie needs a break as well. Incentives to progress are fine but not if they lead to being stressed out when something gets in the way. You all need a bit of fun.'

'What can we do? I suppose if I get desperate enough they'll put Freddie into foster-care or even hospitalise him for a week or two. But he'd hate it and I couldn't enjoy myself, knowing how unhappy he'd be. Or wondering whether he was being properly cared for.'

'Isn't there somewhere he can go for his own holiday? Somewhere he'd really look forward to going to? A special camp for disabled children, maybe.'

'Recreational trips are organised through the school but they're only ever for the day. I've heard of camps but they're too far away and he'd hate being sent off to strangers.'

Anna rested her head back against the tree trunk.

'You know what I'd do if I was the richest person in the world?'

Judith smiled at Anna's dreamy tone. 'No, what?'

'I'd build a camp. Holiday heaven for handicapped kids. Somewhere they only came to have fun. No schoolwork, no occupational therapy, no physiotherapy unless they needed it purely for their physical well-being. They could come on a regular basis for a week or two a couple of times a year so they'd know where they were going and it would be something wonderful they'd look forward to. Some place that's just for them, to give them the independence of going somewhere of their own.'

'What would they do?'

'There'd be a purpose built swimming pool.' Anna smiled. 'With a wave-maker and lots of toys. And a lake with specially adapted boats, a specially designed golf course and an adventure playground. Heaps of music and books and lots of animals. Donkeys and ponies they could ride, cats and dogs to play with and maybe a huge aviary they could get inside.'

'You sound like you've got it all planned.'

'Mmm. We'd have picnics and a special bus for outings. Campfires to tell ghost stories around and enough staff so that children could always have someone with them, day and night.'

'Imagine what it would cost! Think of the staff you'd need.'

'I have.' Anna waved at Nicholas who was now pushing a hand mower across the expanse of lawn. 'We'd need nurses, physios, house mothers and fathers, domestic staff, cooks and administrative staff— and it would be nice to have a doctor available. A director, too, of course.'

'You?'

'I wish.' Anna sighed. 'I love being with the children here but it's all so intensive. So directed to helping the children make progress—like the mobility assessment for Freddie and the prizes for achieving goals. I'd rather help them just have fun.'

'It'll never happen,' Judith said sadly. 'But wouldn't it be perfect? People like me could have a real holiday with the rest of the family, knowing that Freddie was probably having an even better time on his own holiday.'

'It could happen,' Anna said wistfully. 'I've read about places like that in other countries. Like Britain. I'd like to see them.'

'Maybe that's what you should do,' Judith suggested. 'I'm sure you'd get a job in a place like that. The children love you. Freddie is as funny as a fit trying to sing some of your songs at home. Specially that one about a teapot.'

'Coffee-pot.' Anna chuckled then confessed, 'I have been thinking of a job in a place like that. Rather a lot, in fact. But I doubt they'd employ an inexperienced doctor and I don't want to give up medicine entirely.'

'There must be someway you could do both,' Judith decided. 'But not here, unfortunately. We'd all miss you if you went away.'

Anna stood up, stretching her legs. 'Come on, let's go and see how Freddie's getting on. Maybe I can teach you the song about the coffee-pot.'

The notes Mike had been making hadn't been added to for ten minutes. It was a review Mike was concerned about. He'd come into Chandler House that afternoon with the intention of seriously considering the problems eleven-year-old Sophie was having with her mobility. She'd given up even trying to use her calipers and crutches and now refused to get out of her wheelchair. Mike was due to examine her thoroughly to see whether further surgery might be of benefit, but his review of her extensive notes had been halted by the drift of conversation coming through the open window of the office he was using.

He hadn't intended eavesdropping but the familiar tones of Anna's voice had been irresistible. When the two woman moved away from their position under the tree, still chatting, Mike stared after them. He couldn't let Anna leave the country. To leave him— and Nicholas. But what could he do? If he tried to persuade her to stay she'd rebel—refuse to be boxed in and prevented from following a dream which was clearly one she had begun to cherish. Judith Higgs was right. There had to be a way that would allow Anna to have what she most wanted. And he was probably the only person who might be able to do something about it.

Maybe his eavesdropping had provided the perfect inspiration.

CHAPTER EIGHT

'ON THE count of three. One, two, three!'

Anna helped lift her corner of the stretcher, transferring their patient to the bed in the resuscitation area. She was only half listening to the ambulance officer's description of the car accident. The paramedics had been unable to find a vein that hadn't collapsed and it was Anna's priority to establish IV access. The young man hadn't received any pain relief as yet and he was conscious and distressed.

'Wayne?' James Hean was at the head of the bed. 'Was it a head-on collision, mate?'

'No. I think it came from the side. The other car was coming too fast around the corner. It lost control.'

'Were you driving?'

'Yeah.' Wayne made a noise somewhere between a groan and a laugh. 'I was taking this car for a test drive, would you believe?'

'Were you wearing a seat belt?'

'I don't think so. No.'

Anna gave up looking for a vein in Wayne's left arm. 'He's completely shut down,' she told the registrar worriedly. It was a sign of possibly severe internal bleeding. Blood supply to the vital organs was being preserved by closing down the peripheral circulation.

'Keep hunting,' James told her calmly. 'You'll find something. Otherwise we can do a venous cut-down.'

Anna moved around the foot of the bed. Both

Wayne's legs were in Hare traction splints and a large laceration on the right thigh was covered with blood-stained padding. There wasn't going to be any venous access easily available below the waist. She reached Wayne's right arm but the youth groaned loudly.

'Don't touch my arm! Oh, God!' He held the arm flexed tightly over his chest.

'You arm's pretty sore, is it?' James had moved down to the foot of the bed.

'Yeah. And my right chest.'

'Can you straighten this arm?' Anna asked.

'Dunno.'

'Let's try,' Anna urged gently. 'We need to get a drip into you and give you something for the pain.'

'Do both your legs hurt?' James had lifted the padding on Wayne's right thigh.

'Yeah. The right one hurts more.'

'Does it hurt down here?' James was palpating the lower left leg.

'Not much. It feels kind of numb.'

Anna gave up on Wayne's arms. She asked a nurse to support the patient's head and unfastened the cervical collar he was wearing. Touching his neck, she felt a wave of relief.

'I've found a vein,' she told James triumphantly.

'Good girl.' James paused to give Anna an encouraging smile. 'Get a line in and start some fluids.'

'Don't move your head, Wayne,' Anna instructed. 'There's going to be a bit of a jab but you musn't move even if it hurts.' Anna swabbed the side of his neck and reached for a cannula. 'Keep a good hold,' she warned the nurse. 'We don't know what's going on with his neck yet.'

James was tapping on Wayne's chest. Anna wasn't

sure if the shouts of pain were due to that or her insertion of the cannula.

'Take some slow, deep breaths,' James ordered. 'You've got a few broken ribs here, mate. I think you might have come off worse than the steering-wheel.'

The broken ribs were a worry. They were quite likely to pierce the lungs and cause a major problem. 'His breathing's pretty stable right now but I want the ICU reg. down here.' James and Anna had moved out of the way of the X-ray equipment and staff. 'And call Orthopaedics. He's got a lot of repair work for them.'

Anna made the call. It was Ken who came to examine the X-rays.

'You were on take yesterday,' Anna commented.

'It's really the ''Jaws'' team on today,' Ken told her, 'but the man himself has taken a week's leave. Erica and I are taking turns in the cover for Tim. He's not that happy at being landed with the extra load.' Ken shook his head. 'We're going to need a rod for the right femur and plating for the left. His right arm's not pretty either.'

'Is he sick?' Anna felt a sudden wave of alarm.

'He's not well. Looks like half a dozen broken ribs here.'

'Not him. Mr Smith.'

'Sick? No—sharks never get sick.' Ken grinned. 'He's a machine. Never been known to take a day's sick leave in the entire history of the department.' Ken looked at Anna thoughtfully. 'Mind you, he's never been known to take a week's unexpected leave either.' The registrar began to collect the X-ray plates. 'We'll send young Wayne up to ICU for a bit, I think.

We'll wait until we know how stable his chest is before we start turning him into the bionic man.'

Anna found her thoughts gravitating back to Mike at every spare moment throughout the day. It was so out of character. He wouldn't shirk his responsibilities and leave his patients to the care of another team without a very good reason. And what about his private clinics, both here and in Auckland? Anna knew the waiting list for people trying to get their children under his care was huge. Mike had often hinted that his general orthopaedic work in the hospital frustrated his desire to spend more time with these children. He appeared to handle the pressure by working longer hours to try and make the time. Perhaps the pressure had finally had an effect?

What if something terrible had happened? Some crisis in the part of his life Anna had never been allowed to be privy to? It was none of her business now but Anna felt it should be. If Mike needed comfort of some kind then it was she who should provide it. Surely nobody else loved him as much as she did. The thought that he might be in trouble was so upsetting that Anna found it difficult to concentrate. She was very relieved when her shift finally ended but the time to herself only accelerated her train of thought.

She had to do something. Perhaps this was the opportunity she'd thought would never come—to try and back down from her ultimatum and to at least open a new door of communication between them. Anna rang the hospital telephone operator.

'This is Dr Kessel,' she explained. 'I need Mr Michael Smith's home telephone number.'

'I'm sorry, we're not allowed to give out that information.'

'It's a medical matter,' Anna lied. 'It's urgent.'

'Mr Smith is unavailable for the remainder of the week.' The operator sounded pleased with her inside knowledge. 'Mr McPherson is covering. I can page him for you.'

'No, thanks.' Anna groaned inwardly. 'Mr Smith has a cellphone. Do you have that number?'

'We're not allowed to give out that information,' the operator repeated in a bored tone. 'I'll page Mr McPherson for you.'

'It doesn't matter,' Anna responded wearily.

'I thought you said it was urgent?'

'I'll deal with it myself.' Anna put the phone down and then stared at it. She could try Erica Savage. Maybe Mike had given his senior registrar some idea of his whereabouts. Or she could try Charlotte Berry. No, she couldn't do that. What if there was something between her and Mike? Anna didn't want to find out by appearing to be chasing the surgeon. Stuck for ideas, Anna paced her small room. She didn't even know where he lived. Where would he go if he needed time to himself? Suddenly Anna had another idea. She picked up the phone again and rang for a taxi.

The route was familiar but not one that Anna had travelled for what seemed a very long time. As the taxi driver pulled up beside the beach house Anna's first thought was that he could at least have arranged for someone to mow the lawns. The gardens were a magnificent blaze of colour but the unkempt grass made them appear neglected. The weeds had flourished in the well-fertilised soil and the unfinished pathways looked abandoned.

'That'll be thirty dollars,' the taxi driver told her.

But Anna didn't move. The house was clearly deserted, windows tightly shut and blinds drawn. It was the sign on the fence that really shocked her, however. FOR SALE it said, in bold black lettering. A description of the desirable beachfront property appeared under the heading in smaller print but was now largely obscured by the diagonal sign pasted over it. Huge red lettering. SOLD.

'I'll go back to town, now, thanks,' Anna told the driver quietly. 'There's nothing here for me after all.'

Sold. Disposed of. Eliminated from one's life. It was ridiculous to identify herself with a piece of real estate but Anna had given a lot of herself to the beach house property. And to its owner. He must have wanted no reminders of their time together.

What had happened to her guitar? Not that Anna felt the remotest desire to make music for her own sake these days, even though she knew very well its restorative powers for a bruised soul. Perhaps she deserved to be unhappy. She should have given Mike more time. He'd been right. She needed to learn to compromise as much as he did. She'd thought their relationship too important to compromise on. Perhaps Mike had things in his own life that he felt were too important to compromise on as well. She should have waited, instead of handing out accusations and an ultimatum.

Anna's misery fed on itself the next day. The cases she saw in the emergency department seemed tailor-made to make her spirits plummet even further. A child had been knocked down on a pedestrian crossing.

'How old is she?' Anna asked the nurse who had taken the incoming ambulance radio transmission.

'About seven or eight. The police are trying to locate her family.'

'How bad?'

'Femur, chest and head injuries. Query pelvic involvement. Doesn't sound good.'

Anna agreed. The contact point of a car's bumper changed with the size of a person struck. It might miss a crawling baby completely, hit the trochanter of a young child, be at femur level around age six or seven and then down to the tibial plateau of an adult. When the speed of a vehicle was sufficient then the victim was hit in the thorax by the bonnet of the car before being thrown, often with the head making first contact with the road.

The A and E consultant took charge of the profoundly shocked child on arrival. Senior registrars from both the emergency and intensive care departments were assisting so there was little Anna could do. She also had a waiting room filled with other cases for attention. The emergency was uppermost in everybody's mind, even those who weren't directly associated with the resuscitation efforts. Equipment and staff were moving calmly but with a speed that denoted increasing urgency.

Anna dealt with a baby with a severe ear infection, a man with a nasty dog bite and a toddler with a pulled elbow. It was a common injury. Anna had seen another case only last week and James Hean had taken advantage of a quiet spell in the department to give her a thorough tutorial. The cause was obvious enough as well. Anna had always cringed when she saw parents swinging a toddler up into their arms by pulling on their wrists or dragging a reluctant child into following them. Now she knew why this had always instinctively bothered her—it was the major cause of pulled elbows. This particular mother looked as though she stood no nonsense from her active three-year-old.

'Shut up, Harry, and let the doctor look at your arm.'

Anna could already tell what the problem was likely to be by the way the child was refusing to move his arm and was holding it slightly flexed and pronated. Harry's loud wails temporarily obliterated the sounds of frantic activity in the resuscitation area next door but Anna had already heard the shout to charge up the defibrillator.

'I'm going to send Harry up for an X-ray,' Anna told his mother. 'I'm pretty sure he's torn a ligament and it's become caught in the elbow joint.'

The mother sniffed. 'Looks paralysed to me.'

Anna had had enough of the woman's belligerent attitude. She wasn't in the mood. 'The usual cause is pulling a child along by the wrist,' she said coolly.

'Are you accusing *me* of doing this to Harry?'

'No.' Anna sighed. Someone making a complaint about her was not something she wanted to deal with right now. 'Not at all. It's a very common injury.' She scribbled out a requisition form. 'The nurse will show you the way to the X-ray department.'

It was a simple enough procedure to reduce the elbow injury. James had shown her last week and had pointed out the miraculous result—a satisfying click, followed by the cessation of the child's tears and the beginnings of arm movement again. It was often achieved by the radiographers as they positioned the arm for the X-ray examination and Anna hoped that would be the case this time. She had no desire to spend much more time with either Harry or his mother.

The silence as her patient left was uneasy. Anna looked into the resuscitation area as she passed. James Hean looked up but the silence had already told Anna the outcome. The registrar was grim-faced. The nursing staff were removing lines and trying to tidy the tiny body that lay on the bed. As Anna looked away she saw the consultant in the company of an ashen-faced woman, presumably the girl's mother. Anna felt the prickle of tears as the tragedy sank in. She heard the low tones of the consultant's voice as he took the woman into a side-room.

'She had massive internal bleeding, Mrs Cooper. And severe head injuries. We did everything we possibly could to save her. I'm terribly sorry.'

When Anna walked out into the brilliant mid-afternoon sunshine when her shift ended that day it seemed totally inappropriate to the suffering she'd left behind and to her own state of mind. She knew it would be only too easy to retreat to her room and give in to the misery she was feeling so she made a serious effort to overcome the inclination. She decided to go to Chandler House. She needed the comfort of the sound of children's laughter and a dose of their contagious courage to face the obstacles life threw at them.

But, having made the effort to get to her destination, Anna found she couldn't quite face the children. Instead, she found an isolated part of the gardens and sat down under a shady tree. She knew what it was she really needed and that was simply unavailable. She'd seen to that herself.

Half an hour later Nicholas shambled up to Anna's refuge. She accepted the small bunch of scarlet dahlias with mixed emotions and had to blink hard and sniff to stop tears forming. She tried to smile at Nicholas but failed.

'Sorry, Nicky. I love my flowers. It's the nicest thing that's happened all day.'

Nicholas crouched awkwardly beside her. 'Why are you sad?' he managed eventually.

'There was a little girl at the hospital today,' Anna explained. 'She got hit by a car and badly hurt. She…died.' Anna sniffed again. 'It made me sad.'

Nicholas nodded. They sat in silence for a minute and Anna hoped she hadn't upset the boy with her story.

'It's awfully hot today, isn't it?' Anna tried to sound more cheerful. 'Why don't we go and get an ice cream?'

'Where?'

'There must be a shop around here somewhere. Or better yet—let's go to the beach!'

Nicky's eyes lit up then he looked doubtful. 'I'm not allowed.'

'Let's go and ask Miss Berry.' Anna scrambled to her feet and held out her hand. It felt good to have a plan of action, however trivial.

Charlotte also looked doubtful. 'I'm not sure,' she told them. 'It's not something we would usually allow.'

'Nicholas is an employee, not a pupil,' Anna reminded her. 'And I'll take full responsibility. You know me well enough.'

'It's nearly four o'clock. His guardian will be here to collect him at 5.30.'

'We'll be back by then,' Anna promised. 'There's a bus stop just down the road. Please, Charlotte. We're both in dire need of a bit of fun and rules are made to be broken occasionally.'

Nicholas was as excited by the bus ride as any three-year-old. He laughed frequently and talked very loudly. If he noticed the curious stares of other passengers it didn't seem to bother him. At the beach Anna bought them both the largest-sized ice creams available. Then she got Nicholas to hold hers while she took off his boots and socks and rolled up his trousers. They both walked through the shallow surf, their footwear in one hand, ice creams in the other.

Anna began to feel more relaxed than she had in a long time. Her companion's pleasure in the small treat was delightful, the sunshine, surf and crowd of people out simply to enjoy themselves created a carefree atmosphere that was a very welcome change.

'Do you ever have holidays, Nicky?' Anna asked suddenly.

Nicholas nodded, his mouth full of chocolate ice-cream which had also managed to spread itself over half his face.

'I mean real holidays. Not just time off work. Going away somewhere just to have fun.'

Nicholas nodded again and grinned, more ice-cream escaping to land on his white T-shirt in a large blob.

'Where do you go?'

Nicholas struggled with the difficult word but Anna waited patiently. Finally she understood. 'Pauanui?

That's a great place. I went camping there. Do you go camping?'

'No.'

'Where do you stay?'

Nicholas swallowed the last of his ice-cream cone. He wiped his face with his hand, then wiped his hand on his T-shirt. 'With my old foster-family,' he said quite clearly. 'They shifted and every year I go for two weeks. They're nice.'

Anna smiled. Nicky's face and T-shirt had matching brown smudges. 'How long did you live with them?' she asked gently.

'Since I was born.' Nicholas watched a wave coming towards them. 'My mother didn't want me.'

Anna led Nicholas back towards the dry sand. His trouser leg had come unrolled and was now very wet. 'That's sad, Nicky. I'm sorry about that.'

'She's dead now.' He sounded matter-of-fact, unimpressed by either his mother's life or death. Anna wondered how deeply he might feel the rejection he was clearly aware of but didn't want to pry into a sensitive area.

'We'd better get our shoes back on,' she decided. 'We'll have to catch the bus again soon.' She struggled with Nicky's large feet as she eased the orthopaedic footwear back on. It wasn't a task he could manage himself. 'Who looks after you now, Nicky?'

'Mrs Martin. She's nice. And my…my…'

'Mr Martin?' Anna offered.

Nicholas hesitated then nodded. 'He's nice, too.'

Anna smiled. Nicholas had a child's acceptance and generosity towards the people he knew well. They were all 'nice'. She assumed the Martins were also foster-parents and was glad Nicholas still had contact with the family that had taken him in at birth. His history of foster-care must be a lot happier than that of many children, particularly disabled ones.

They had to wait ten minutes for a bus on the return route but they weren't too late. Anna was more worried about the state of cleanliness in which she was returning Nicholas.

'You look like you had a fight with the ice cream, instead of eating it,' Anna told him. 'Was it fun?'

'Yeah!' Nicholas laughed.

They were both laughing as they turned into the gates of Chandler House. The minibuses that delivered the children home were long gone, as were most of the staff. The car park was nearly empty. Just Charlotte Berry's car and a black BMW. Anna's heart leapt at seeing Mike but her smile faded almost instantly. He looked absolutely furious.

'Just where the *hell* have you been?' he snapped.

'The beach. We went to get an ice cream.' Anna felt flustered.

'Why did you take Nicholas?' Mike's expression was stony, his tone accusing.

'He wanted an ice cream as well.' Anna bridled at the accusing tone. 'Why on earth should it bother you?'

Mike turned towards Nicholas who was looking dismayed and confused. 'Get your things, Nicholas. It's time to go home.' He swung back to glare at Anna. 'How could you do that? Parade him around like some sort of worthy cause? Invite public ridicule. The beach must have been packed on a day like this.'

'Yes, it was.' Anna was also confused but she was beginning to feel angry as well. 'And, yes, of course some people stared at us. But Nicky wasn't bothered and neither was I. If people want to react that way then that's their problem. Why should people like Nicholas be shut away before he offends their sensibilities?'

'For their own protection,' Mike snapped.

'You're as bad as any of them, then,' Anna retorted angrily. Her voice rose. 'It's just another little box for you, isn't it, Mike? Disabled people are fine but only if they're safely contained in their institutions or on a properly supervised and protected outing.'

'It's Nicholas I'm concerned about. He needs the security. What he doesn't need is public scrutiny, disapproval or pity. And he doesn't need someone singling him out for attention in order to make them feel better about themselves.'

Anna was outraged. 'How dare you suggest I took Nicky out for some ulterior motive of being seen as some sort of do-gooder? I happen to enjoy his company.' She lowered her voice. 'And I think he enjoys mine.'

'Yes, he does.' Mike also sounded calmer. 'And that's part of the problem, isn't it?'

'What are you talking about?'

'He's very fond of you, Anna. He doesn't trust people easily and when he loves them it's a serious commitment. Just how do you think he's going to cope when you walk out on his life? The way you walked out on mine. Do you make a habit of breaking hearts?'

'I didn't want to walk out, Mike. It was the last thing I wanted.' Anna's tone was vehement. She took a deep breath. 'Let him cross his own bridges, Mike. You tried to box me in and now you're trying to do the same to Nicky. You may be his doctor but you have no right to interfere with his personal life.'

'I have every right,' Mike informed her coolly. 'Nicholas Smith is my brother.'

CHAPTER NINE

IT ALL made sense.

Not a senile grandparent or a mad aunt and certainly not a vicious dog. Michael Smith had been hiding a handicapped sibling. Initially too stunned to respond to Mike's admission, Anna had watched him walk away from her. She'd thought of little else since.

Had Mike kept the relationship hidden from her because he was ashamed of his brother? Or did he think that Anna would be unable to accept Nicholas and that it would damage their relationship? Anna veered from feeling angry with Mike's over-protectiveness and secrecy to feeling insulted by his supposed assumption of her reaction. And why had he apparently refused to accept that her friendship with Nicholas was genuine during their confrontation after the beach outing yesterday? Confusion had to be added to the medley of other emotions.

A sneaking sympathy crept in at some point, however. Many people *were* put off by close association with severely disabled people and having one in the family was a very different matter to simply working with them. If the positions had been reversed would she have wanted a fragile new relationship exposed to such a challenge?

Mike had never mentioned his father. His mother was dead and had been unable or had chosen not to be a parent to Nicholas in any case. Mike had clearly assumed a parenting role for his much younger sibling. It was quite normal for any parent to feel protective. Those feelings had to be magnified when the child was disabled. And he was right. Anna hadn't given enough thought to the repercussions of encouraging a friendship with Nicholas. It was Mike who'd have to pick up the pieces if she unintentionally caused his brother to be hurt.

It was like an echo of her own thoughts when she overheard the name of Chandler House in the emergency department the next morning. Anna stopped abruptly on her way to administer a tetanus booster to a builder who'd come in with a rusty nail embedded in his foot.

'What's that about Chandler House?'

'There's a patient on the way in,' James explained. 'A chap had some sort of turn while he was up a ladder. Sounds like he's broken his arm but the ambulance officers are more concerned about a possible arrhythmia and brief loss of consciousness.'

'Who is it?' Anna asked, feeling the colour drain from her face.

'An ex-pupil, I believe. Nicholas something. He's got cerebral palsy.'

'Smith?' Anna gasped. 'Nicholas Smith?'

'That's it. How could I forget a name like that?' James looked more closely at Anna. 'Do you know him?'

'Yes. Has his family been informed?'

'Couldn't say. The centre's director is coming in with him. Apparently he's pretty agitated. We'll probably need to sedate him.'

Anna put down the kidney dish containing the syringe she had been carrying. 'I'll be back in a minute.'

The telephone she chose was well away from the

main desk. 'Mike? This is Anna. Nicholas is being brought into A and E.'

'I know. Charlotte rang me. She's coming in with him.'

'You can get down here before he arrives if you hurry.'

There was a moment's silence. Then Mike spoke quietly. 'My family business is not really something I want gossiped about, Anna. Charlotte has the authority to act as next-of-kin. She'll stay with him.'

'You can't be serious.' Now Anna was convinced Mike kept his brother hidden for personal motives. 'Why? Are you ashamed of your brother?'

'No, it's not that,' Mike said quickly, but Anna's temper was roused.

'I hope not,' she snarled into the phone, 'because if it is then he'd have far more reason to be ashamed of *you*. You should be proud of Nicholas, Mike. He's a wonderful person and he's achieving what he wants out of life against all the odds. Now he's hurt and he needs you. Why can't you forget whatever selfish standpoint you've taken and do the right thing?' Anna had no idea she was shouting. 'Get out of your box, Mike. Get a life!' She slammed down the phone and swung around to face the astonished gaze of James Hean. He was carrying the kidney dish she'd abandoned. Anna took it off him then saw the stretcher arriving. She handed the dish and syringe to a passing nurse.

'Cubicle four,' she told her. 'The guy who had the nail in his foot. He can go home as soon as he's had this tetanus jab.'

Anna raced to intercept the stretcher but had to wait while Nicholas was transferred to the bed. The boy

was distressed and shouting loudly. He'd been re-
strained in the ambulance but the straps were undone
now as staff moved him. Anna dodged past the ambulance officer who was holding the unbroken arm
firmly pinned down.

'Nicky? It's Anna. It's all right. I'll look after you.'

But Nicholas couldn't hear Anna over the roaring
noise he was making. James ordered a sedative. There
was no way they could get any ECG electrodes on to
monitor any arrhythmia at present.

'He was only unconscious for about a minute,' the
ambulance officer shouted above the uproar. 'No sign
of head injury and a witness said it looked as though
he fainted while up the ladder.'

'He's got a congenital heart condition.' Anna recognised Charlotte Berry's calm tones. 'A ventricular
septal defect that was corrected but he's prone to
SVTs. He's had syncopal episodes in the past.'

Anna didn't have time to be impressed by
Charlotte's knowledge of an employee's medical history or to wonder whether she was that clued up on
all her pupils. She was still trying to make Nicholas
recognise her. She leaned over and touched his face.
'Nicky—it's me, Anna.'

Suddenly the ambulance officer lost his grip on
Nicholas's arm. With a strength magnified by des-
peration Nicholas swung the arm in a curve that
ended in contact with Anna's cheek-bone. The force
of the blow knocked her backwards and she landed
in a crumpled heap against a nest of IV poles.

'Where the hell is that Valium?' she heard James
shout.

Dazed, Anna shook her head, becoming aware of
the sharp pain on the left side of her face. Strong

hands raised her to a sitting position and gentle fingers were probing at the sore area. Anna's eyes were screwed tightly shut but tears of pain still managed to ooze from the corners.

'Nothing broken.' She heard the verdict given. 'Thank God for that.'

Astonishment broke through the pain. Anna opened her eyes to see a face very close to her own. Tawny eyes with golden glints that looked at her with grave concern. She felt herself being lifted to her feet, but the hands supporting her didn't let go. 'You'd better get some ice on that, my love. You're going to have a nasty black eye.'

She must have hit her head as well, Anna decided. There was no way she could be hearing correctly. Mr Michael Smith calling her 'my love' in front of professional colleagues? But a glance towards those colleagues confirmed her own impression of the unusual. The IV Valium had calmed Nicholas miraculously. Nursing staff had already wired him up to monitor his heart rhythm and blood pressure and James was splinting the obviously broken arm. They were all busy but seemed to be managing to stare at the orthopaedic consultant and his unexpected patient at the same time. Charlotte had a knowing but rather satisfied smile on her face.

'Are you OK, Anna?' James Hean wasn't quite gaping at them but it was a close call.

'I'm fine,' Anna replied. She took a step then realised that Mike still had his arm around her. No wonder everybody was staring! 'I need to talk to Nicholas,' she said. 'To let him know I'm here.'

'You get some ice on that eye,' Mike told her. 'I'll look after Nicholas.' Mike's chin went up firmly.

'Nicholas Smith is my brother,' he told the A and E staff. 'I can fill you in on his cardiac history and I'd like to supervise the treatment for his arm, if I may.'

The rest of the department looked as dazed as Anna felt as she went off in search of an ice-pack. She was still sitting, holding it against her cheek, thirty minutes later when Mike came to find her.

'Nicholas is fine,' he told her. 'It's a straightforward fracture which should heal well. He's going up to the coronary care unit for monitoring after he's got his cast on. He's in A-Fib which should settle spontaneously but he might need a shock to get him back into sinus rhythm.'

'Is it a life-threatening condition?'

'Potentially.' Mike smiled gently. 'Some people have been surprised Nicky's made it as far as he has. I've cared for him for ten years now and losing him is a possibility I've always lived with. Maybe that's one reason I didn't tell you about him. Maybe I thought that if I could keep our relationship simple for long enough it wasn't a responsibility I'd have to involve you with.'

'Maybe it's a responsibility I'd like to have been involved with,' Anna said. 'Did that ever occur to you?'

'Not soon enough, obviously.' Mike chewed at his lip thoughtfully. 'James thinks you should take the rest of your shift off. To look after your eye.'

'I'm fine,' Anna insisted.

'Well, take an hour off, then,' Mike said persuasively. 'Charlotte's staying with Nicholas while he gets his cast on and goes up to CCU. He's happy. There's something I'd like to show you. I'll pick you up in my car in ten minutes.'

Anna hesitated for a long moment.

'Please, Anna?'

'OK. At the side-entrance, I suppose?'

'No way. At the front door.' Mike's lips quirked in an almost embarrassed manner as he turned away. 'I'm just going to tell Nicky we'll be back in an hour or so.'

If the staff in A and E had been shocked by Michael Smith's familiarity with a colleague then the front desk receptionists and the orderlies were even more surprised when the black BMW pulled up on the 'No Parking' dotted yellow lines. Michael Smith got out of his car, still wearing his white coat, and held the passenger door open for Anna Kessel, also still wearing her white coat. She looked as if she'd had her face slapped rather hard, they decided later, but she also looked quite happy to be getting into the consultant surgeon's car. And hadn't he been observed carrying a large bouquet of flowers into the hospital quite recently?

For some reason Anna expected Mike to head to the beach so she was surprised when he drove them up into the hills that bordered the south side of the township above Welcome Bay and kept going past where the housing subdivisions ended. She'd been listening to Mike talk about his brother and knew she'd been very wrong in accusing him of being ashamed of the relationship.

'But you're not entirely wrong,' Mike said in response to her apology. 'I was once. I didn't even know Nicholas existed until a solicitor called me in to settle my mother's estate. Amongst the papers were his birth certificate and documents concerning his availability for adoption.' Mike sighed heavily and was silent for a minute. He turned the car off the main road onto what looked like a tractor path across a grassy paddock but he continued to drive, very slowly.

'Nobody adopted him, of course, but my mother was able to offer enough of a financial incentive to find excellent foster-care, fortunately. She could pay her way out of her inconvenience.' Mike's tone was disgusted.

'How did she keep it hidden from you?' Anna wondered aloud.

Mike laughed without amusement. 'I was a bit of an inconvenience myself. I was born when my mother was quite young—in her early twenties. Before her career took off. I got sent to boarding school when I was seven and I never saw much of her after that. Her career took priority.'

'What did she do?'

'She was in the rag trade,' Mike explained. 'Started with one shop, which expanded into a nationwide chain. Then she moved into the Australian market and that was so successful she started up in Europe. She was named businessperson of the year several times. The car accident that killed her was in North America. She'd gone to negotiate a deal to get into the market there.'

Anna nodded slowly as Mike finally brought the car to a halt. They were on the crest of a hill and the land stretched out in a gentle slope before them. The view was astounding. The city lay to their left, the outlines of the harbour, estuaries and bays looking like pieces of a complicated jigsaw puzzle. The cone of Mount Maunganui sat in its distinctive isolation, terminating the huge, unbroken stretch of beach. The islands and distant hilly coastline of the Coromandel Peninsula bordered a scene straight from a picture postcard. They both sat in an absorbed silence for a minute. Then Anna spoke softly.

'I think I can understand why you don't like the idea of career women having children,' she said. 'You must have felt unwanted. But what about your father?'

'He was an inconvenience, too, I suspect,' Mike said quietly. 'He died just after Nicholas was born. I think there were some suspicions that his death wasn't an accident but it got hushed up. I went home for the funeral but wasn't told anything. As I said, I never found out I had a brother until Mother was killed.'

'Why did she have another baby?' Anna asked. 'If she already had no time for her family.'

'It wasn't intentional.' Mike was staring at the view before them. 'I did some digging after she died and found the doctor she went to. She was in her early forties at that stage and was so busy establishing her empire that she had no idea she was pregnant until it was far too late to consider a termination. She still tried and managed to bring on labour but ran into trouble. They hospitalised her, controlled her labour and Nicholas was born a few weeks later at twenty-eight weeks' gestation. Brain damaged and with other problems like hydrocephalus and heart defects. She refused to take him home.' Mike unclipped his safety belt. 'Come on, I want to show you something.'

Anna followed Mike across the paddock towards the bush line where the slope flattened out. It was then she noticed the small river running through the trees.

'This is beautiful, Mike.'

'The river broadens out down here. It's almost a lake—or could be if it was enlarged a bit.' Mike strode ahead, the corners of his white coat flapping, and Anna hurried to catch up.

'What did you mean—I wasn't entirely wrong?' Anna queried breathlessly. 'You obviously decided to make up for your mother's treatment of Nicholas when you did find out.'

'I was horrified when I first met him,' Mike admitted. 'He was only six, very backward and hyperactive. I'd never had anything to do with handicapped people and it was a total shock to think that Nicholas and I were related. But his foster-mother, Bronwyn, was wonderful. She brought us together and made me part of the family as well. I came to Tauranga as a house surgeon myself so I could spend more time with them. That's when Nicky started at Chandler House and really started to make some progress. It was then that I took Nicky to live with me and employed the Martins as housekeepers and caregivers. They've really become another set of foster-parents.

'Then Bronwyn and her husband decided to retire to Pauanui. Nicky still goes to see them every year for a holiday and I go as well but try to get some time to myself. A day or two on my own.'

'Like a camping trip into Broken Hills?' Anna smiled.

'Exactly.'

'Why didn't you give me a chance, Mike? You knew I thought you were shutting me out of an important part of your life. Why couldn't you tell me about Nicky?'

'I was engaged once,' Mike admitted. 'I thought that she loved me enough to share the responsibility

I wanted to take on with Nicky. I took her to meet him. I expected her to be shocked—I had been myself—but I thought that she might accept him when she got to know him. Might even come to love him, as I did by then.'

'But she didn't?'

'She never tried. She wanted nothing to do with him. But what really hurt was that she told me she'd never have my children. She wasn't going to risk producing another monster. That's what she called him.'

'Oh, Mike.' Anna shook her head. 'That's awful!' Then she frowned. 'You really thought I might feel the same way?'

'Not exactly. But I was afraid to lose you, Anna. I couldn't bring myself to take any risk, however small it might be.'

'But even when it was obvious that Nicky and I were friends you accused me of some ulterior motive. How could you, Mike? That really hurt.'

'I'm still trying to work that out,' Mike confessed. 'I was really shaken that day to find you at Chandler House. Parts of my life were being mixed up when I'd worked so hard to keep them separate. I felt I was losing control. I needed time to re-adjust. That's why I walked out on our argument. It was me that needed the time to think, not you.'

'And I thought you had something going with Charlotte Berry.' Anna smiled. 'She's just your type, according to Ken Slater.'

'Is that right?'

'Mmm.' Anna was encouraged by the amusement she saw in Mike's eyes. 'So's Erica Savage. Strong, competent women with no desire to mix a career and children.'

'Exactly why I wouldn't be interested,' Mike smiled. 'They're like my mother was—or should have been.' He shook his head. 'I suppose I shouldn't generalise. It's been too easy to assume that successful career women are potentially bad wives and mothers.'

'And to assume that someone wanting to share your life would be put off by Nicholas?'

Mike nodded. 'I think I had to play devil's advocate to convince myself that it was really true. That you really cared about Nicholas even when you had no idea he was my brother.'

'And were you convinced?'

Mike nodded again. 'When I knew how my fiancée felt all those years ago, it changed my life. That's when I really made the commitment to Nicholas and when I directed my career towards working with other handicapped children. I started supporting Chandler House financially. It was rather satisfying to use some of Mother's money for that.'

'I suppose she had rather a lot,' Anna commented.

'Millions. Tens of millions, in fact. It's all sitting in a trust fund at present,' Mike told her. 'The interest alone is more than enough to run a place like Chandler House.' He smiled broadly. 'But I just spent a bit more. I took a few days off last week to look for something and I found just what I was looking for. When I knew how you really felt yesterday I made a decision to change my life again. To get a life, in fact, as you suggested I should this morning.' Mike reached out to touch Anna's bruised cheek with a gentle finger.

'I didn't take Nicky straight home after your beach trip. I called my solicitor and made him stay late to sign a contract, finalising the purchase I was considering.'

'What was it?' Anna was intrigued. She knew that the change Mike was making somehow included her. Otherwise, why would he be telling her all this, sweeping aside the boundaries that had shut her out of his life? And why would they be standing on the top of this remote hill, looking slightly ridiculous in their white coats? She tried to hold back the bubble of hope but failed completely. Mike was grinning at her, keeping up the suspense. 'Tell me what you've bought, Mike,' Anna ordered.

'This!' Mike's arm swept in a wide circle. 'One hundred acres of it. Wonderful view, forest, river, potential lake. Perfect!'

'It's wonderful,' Anna agreed. 'Are you going to live here?'

'Sure am. I think the best site for a house is over there.' Mike pointed back to where the car was parked. 'Up the hill a bit so it'll look down on the river and lake and the rest of the buildings.'

'The rest of the buildings?' Anna echoed.

'The accommodation and service areas.' Mike grinned at Anna. He looked like an excited child. 'The place disabled kids are going to dream about coming to for a holiday.'

Anna's mouth dropped open. 'What made you think of doing this?'

'I was eavesdropping,' Mike confessed. He stood close to Anna and put an arm around her shoulders. 'I heard of a dream that somebody had. Someone who has music in her soul and the wisdom to know that life shouldn't be all work and no play. Especially for people that have to work harder than most just to get along.' He turned to face Anna and his gaze was gentle. 'You've broken a few boundaries for me, Anna. And I want to thank you.'

Anna was still stunned. She said nothing and Mike bent forward and kissed her softly. 'We'd better get back. Nicholas will be wondering where we are.'

'He's going to love this plan,' Anna murmured as she got back into the car.

Mike nodded. 'You haven't seen him really interacting with the youngsters. He's a born leader. The Martins are really excited about it, too. They'll be the first house parents. I just hope Nicholas lives long enough to see it become a reality.'

'I hope so, too,' Anna said fervently. 'Will it take long, do you think?'

Mike nodded. 'Two to three years at a guess to get it all up and running.' He looked sideways at Anna as he turned the black BMW back onto the main road. 'Long enough for some intensive training for a medically qualified director to take over the whole show.'

'Aren't you going to do that?'

Mike shook his head. 'I'm going to be too busy. That's another change I'm making to the trust fund. It's going to finance my private practice. I intend to go into that full time and give up the general orthopaedic work I'm doing. I've needed it as part of my training but now I'm going to follow my own dream and specialise completely.'

'But that will make it impossible for some people to see you,' Anna said worriedly. 'What about people like Sue Jacobs, who can barely afford her living costs even with part-time work?'

'That's why the trust is going to finance it,' Mike said happily. 'Private care but it's going to be free.

Accessible to everyone. Hey, do you reckon Sue might like a job at the holiday camp? We can build staff quarters with access for children like Emily.'

'I expect she'd love it.' Anna had to smile at Mike's enthusiasm. She waited as he parked the BMW in the consultants' car park and then unclipped her safety belt.

'Wait a minute,' Mike said. 'You haven't told me whether you're interested or not.'

'Interested in what?'

'The position, of course. As director.'

'Are you offering *me* the job?'

'Of course. That's what this little outing has been all about. I can just see you in charge of it all. And when you're not too busy you can sit under a tree in the forest and play your guitar.'

'That could be difficult.'

'Why?'

'I left the guitar at the beach house by mistake,' Anna admitted. 'It's been sold, hasn't it?'

Mike groaned. 'Yes. I wanted to get rid of the final reminders of my mother. I never even went back after you left. The contents of the house all got sent to auction. I'm sorry, Anna.'

'It doesn't matter.' Anna smiled. 'It was a very old guitar.' She opened the car door. 'And, yes, I am interested in the position.' She bit her lip. It was very like the moment she'd agreed to act as caretaker for the beach house, knowing that the position involved much more than any employment duties.

'Is there anything in the fine print I should know about?' Her question was tentative. They both knew what she was really asking.

'Could be.' Mike sounded noncommittal. 'My solicitor is drawing up the contract even as we speak. I'll see that it's delivered as soon as possible. I'd advise you to read it very carefully. Especially the final clause.'

CHAPTER TEN

WOULD it arrive today?

Would it arrive at all, in fact? The contract for Anna's position as caretaker of the beach house property had been mythical. Nothing had been signed and the intimate implications of the 'fine print' had been mutually amusing. But this was serious. It would involve a long-term commitment to the position as director of a large and permanent establishment. Establishment of a personal dream. It was too good to be true. There had to be some sort of a catch.

What could be contained in the final clause that Mike had mentioned specifically? An agreement never to let her position be compromised by personal distractions, perhaps? Like a husband? Or, even worse, children?

Even if it did, Anna knew she'd be only too eager to sign up. The career choice was absolutely right and she was convinced that Mike wanted to re-establish at least the relationship they'd shared previously. Not that that was possible now, of course. The barriers were down. Mike's prejudices and fears had been revealed and their origins were only too understandable.

Maybe it would take time for him to realise that anything was possible as far as their relationship was concerned. That they could cross any bridges as long as they did it together. Anna wasn't concerned at how long it might take. She knew that she needed to learn to compromise a little more herself. She also knew now what she was up against and that the difficulties were surmountable. She could change and Mike had proved himself capable of changing.

No, Anna didn't believe he was really changing. He was merely allowing himself to relax the rigid structure he'd developed in order to protect both his brother and himself. Anna knew the gentleness and passion of which Michael Smith was capable. Maybe now more people would be able to share that knowledge.

It was a day full of promise. It was just a shame she had to go through it looking like she'd been in a prize fight.

'What a shiner!' James Hean whistled in appreciation when Anna appeared on duty. He was standing with Ken Slater in front of the X-ray viewing screens.

'I know.' Anna touched her eye ruefully. 'There didn't seem much point in trying to disguise it. I don't even possess that much make-up.'

'Perhaps you should get an X-ray. That cheek's a bit swollen.'

'It's already been checked.' Anna felt herself reddening. 'A consultant's opinion is good enough for me.'

'Hmm.' James eyed Anna strangely. 'You seem to know Michael Smith rather well.'

'I was his house surgeon for three months,' Anna murmured. 'And I'd met him before that, actually.'

'Really?' Ken's eyes widened dramatically. 'You never told me. Where was that?'

'Swimming.' Anna grinned. She was feeling too good to resist teasing the registrars. She pinched her nostrils together. *'Doo do Doo do Doo do!'*

Ken laughed but James shook his head in confusion. 'We live in strange times,' he told the ceiling. Then he looked at Ken. 'What's this I hear about Smith resigning, Ken?'

'Word through the grapevine is that he offered his resignation yesterday. Going into private practice full time. Have you heard anything, Anna?'

'One or two things,' Anna said evasively. 'I'll bet Erica's delighted. Will she take on the consultant position?'

'I should think so. Tim's retiring at the end of the year so that'll be another spot to fill. And there's more talk of a third consultant. It's going to be a completely new department.' Ken sounded worried.

'Change can be a good thing,' Anna told him cheerfully. Her own optimism wasn't going to be dampened. 'New blood, fresh ideas—a new direction.'

'I'm not so sure.' Ken looked thoughtful. '"Jaws" might have been a bit of a bastard but at least you knew exactly where you were with him. We might even miss having him around. I suspect that underneath it all he's probably quite a nice guy.'

Anna laughed. 'I suspect you're probably right.'

Both men looked at Anna with raised eyebrows but she ignored their unspoken query. 'What's brought you down here, Ken? Anything interesting?' She turned pointedly to gaze at the X-rays. 'That's a great greenstick fracture.'

'Would you like to reduce it?' Ken grinned. 'Four-year-old boy with a bad temper and an inclination to bite.'

'Sounds right up my street,' Anna agreed. 'I'm getting quite experienced at dealing with characters like that.'

'So I've heard.' Ken threw a knowing glance at James Hean and they both smiled. Anna felt herself blushing again.

'What cubicle is he in?' She tried to sound businesslike. 'I think we'd all better get on with some work.'

Anna used a morning tea-break to duck up to the coronary care unit. She heard Nicholas laugh even before she entered the unit and she was delighted to see Mike standing at the end of his brother's bed. Mike nodded and smiled at Anna but continued his conversation with the cardiologist. They were discussing the results of an echocardiogram and changes planned to the medication Nicholas was currently receiving. Anna moved past them as Nicholas laughed again. He was reading a Superman comic.

'Hi, Nicky. You look like you're feeling OK.'

'Hi, Anna. Look!' Nicholas jerked his arm free of the pillow it was resting on. Anna stepped back to avoid contact with the cast. Glancing up, she caught Mike's alarmed gaze but he still didn't break off his conversation.

'Wow!' Anna told Nicholas. 'It's pink!'

'Yeah!' Nicholas grinned. 'They asked me what colour I wanted. I said pink.'

'You sure did.' Anna smiled. Only the tips of his fingers were visible beneath the luridly coloured cast. 'It's neat. Does your arm hurt?'

Nicholas shook his head. 'Not any more.' He was staring at Anna. 'What happened to your eye?'

'I got in the way of something. Like Superman does sometimes.' Anna pointed to a picture in the comic with the large word '*Pow*' above the rather violent depiction of the hero sorting out yet another crisis. She was pleased that Nicholas had no idea he'd been responsible for the injury.

'Wow.' Nicholas was impressed. 'Does it hurt?'

'Not any more.' Anna smiled again. 'Can I write on your arm?'

Nicholas nodded enthusiastically and Anna took a felt-tip pen from her pocket. She looked up at the monitors above the bed as she did so. Snatches of the conversation between the consultants made her confident that Nicky's condition hadn't deteriorated since his last major check-up but it was reassuring to see the normal readings for heart rate, rhythm and blood pressure.

Anna drew a happy face on the pink cast and signed her name. She added a few x's. As she drew the last kiss Anna was aware of the silence at the end of the bed. The cardiologist had gone.

'You'll be able to go home today, Nicky,' Mike informed his brother. 'You can go back to work as well but no tree-pruning or mowing lawns for a few weeks. I've got to do some work now but I'll come and see you when Mrs Martin arrives to take you home.' Mike turned to leave and Anna felt a sharp pang. Wasn't he even going to say hello?

Then Mike turned. His direct gaze held Anna's firmly. 'My office, Dr Kessel. 3 p.m.'

The hours between morning tea and lunchtime went surprisingly quickly. A heart-attack victim, an old lady knocked off her bicycle, the aftermath of an epileptic fit and a ruptured appendix kept Anna far too busy to think about herself or her three o'clock appointment. Given half an hour for a lunch-break,

Anna excused herself from the emergency department. She went into the hospital coffee-shop to buy
a sandwich and when she came out, folding the paper
bag to put in her pocket, she almost walked into the
small wheelchair parked nearby.

'Emily!' she exclaimed. 'Hello, darling!'

The little girl's face lit up. 'Mumma's in the shop,'
she cried happily. 'She's buying a new mouse!'

Sue Jacobs emerged from the gift shop. 'Hi, Anna!'
She held out her purchase. 'Model number three. Just
as well they're not expensive.'

'I could have got that for you. Did you come in
specially?'

'No.' Sue smiled. 'We had an outpatient appointment. Oh, look. You've got to see this.' She reached
into the tray under the seat of the wheelchair and
produced two miniature crutches. 'Let's show Anna
what we showed Mr Smith, Emmy.'

Anna only noticed then that Emily's plasters were
gone. The small legs were now encased in long calipers. Sue lifted her daughter who stood with her arms
locked around her mother's neck while Sue made ad-
justments to the hinged part of the calipers. Emily
grinned at Anna when Sue fitted the tiny crutches
under her arms.

The flow of people around the coffee and gift shops
made a large detour to avoid the small group but a
few slowed and then stopped to watch the little girl.
Emily stood, swaying, as Sue helped her move the
crutches forward one at a time. Then she let go and
Emily swung her legs forward and moved a step. The
process was painfully slow but the toddler's triumphant grin was worth seeing. She wobbled into a fall
after the third step but Anna caught her in her arms.

The spectators clapped but Anna felt close to tears. She hugged the child tightly.

'Clever girl,' she whispered. 'I'm really proud of you.'

Half her lunch break was gone when she waved a farewell to Sue and Emily, but Anna didn't return to the emergency department. Instead, she went into a part of the hospital she'd only recently become familiar with. She ate her sandwich as she walked.

The spinal rehabilitation unit was small, its patients generally in for a long stay, and Tony McLaughlin had become a great favourite with the staff.

'I'm going home next week,' Tony told Anna. 'And guess what? I stood up today.'

'What? I don't believe it!'

'Well, it wasn't quite on my own. I was strapped to that table thing that tilts, you know?'

Anna nodded. 'You've been doing that for a while, haven't you?'

'Yes, but I could never get quite upright. I'd get too dizzy and sick. But today I got my feet on the floor.'

'That's great! How's the arm power?'

'Look at this!' Tony flexed his biceps and Anna made a suitably impressed sound. 'I can almost lift myself in and out of the wheelchair now.'

'Are you still swimming?'

'Yeah. Mum's going to bring me in to physio every day. We always start with a swim.'

'How's the guitar-playing?'

Tony grinned. 'It's a life-saver. I think it's made me quite a popular patient.'

'I think you would have been anyway.' Anna returned his smile. As Erica might have said, Tony had a great attitude.

'Even Mr Smith likes to hear me playing,' Tony told Anna. 'He even asked me all about my guitar when he was in yesterday. He seemed quite impressed. You know, I don't think he's so grumpy after all.'

'No.' Anna grinned. 'And I'm sure he was impressed. You've done really well, Tony.'

'I'm going to walk again,' the youth said with a quiet conviction. 'I've made up my mind. You know, I think you can achieve anything if you're focussed enough.'

'You could be right there. Giving up is certainly the quickest way to fail.'

'Even if you don't make it at least you know you've done your best. But there's not much point doing anything if you expect to fail, is there?'

'Absolutely not,' Anna agreed. 'I have to go, Tony, but I'll be thinking of you. Don't ever stop making music.'

'I won't,' Tony promised. 'Don't you stop, either.'

The hours between lunch and 3 p.m. dragged. In contrast to the morning rush the emergency department was quiet. Too quiet. Anna had too much time to think. As 3 p.m. approached Anna found she was becoming increasingly nervous.

'Why don't you head off?' James suggested. 'You've obviously got something on your mind and we're not exactly pushed around here at the moment. You look more like a patient than a doctor, anyway.'

'OK, thanks.' Anna made a trip to the locker room. She hung up her white coat, unpinned and brushed her hair and applied a fresh coat of pale pink lipstick. The colours of her black eye had deepened during the day. James was right. She did look more like a patient than a doctor. And right now she felt just as nervous as someone waiting for an unpleasant medical procedure.

It took quite an effort to make herself head in the direction of M.G. Smith's office. It was all rather too similar to the first time she'd followed this particular route. Her future was hanging in the balance and it wasn't something she could turn away from. Once again she told herself she might as well bite the bullet and get the nervous anticipation over with.

Her knock on the door went unanswered. So did the second. Anna checked her watch. Two minutes past three. It was out of character for Michael Smith to be unpunctual. Disconcerted, Anna looked around. She caught the gaze of one of the departmental secretaries.

'Mr Smith said just to go in,' the woman called. 'He had to go to an emergency but he'll be back shortly.' The woman's gaze was curious, her smile a little knowing.

Anna nodded. She opened the heavy wooden door to the office and then shut it behind her. She wished she'd left her white coat on. At least the visit might have looked potentially professional. But, then, the gossip had already begun, judging by James's and Ken's comments that morning. If Mike had wanted to stifle it, he wouldn't have invited her to his office.

Not invited—ordered. Anna smiled to herself. Old habits died hard. She stared at the desk in front of her. There was a very large package sitting on the top. Anna stepped closer. A small white card on the brown paper wrapping had her name on it.

An attempt had been made to disguise the shape of the package but Anna knew what it was the moment she touched it. She smiled broadly. Mike must have decided to replace the guitar he'd accidentally sold along with the contents of the beach house. Was that why he'd questioned Tony about his guitar? And what had Tony told him? Anna ripped the paper away. Surely it wasn't...

It was. A Martin guitar. A twelve-string. The most beautiful instrument Anna had ever seen. Awed, she ran her fingers down the neck. It was then she noticed the large white envelope tucked under the base of the strings. Anna moved around the desk, sitting down in Mike's leather chair as she opened the envelope.

In a typically long-winded legal style the document began by detailing the management of the trust fund Mike had told her of. Then there was a whole page setting out the mission statement for the proposed holiday camp. Anna couldn't have worded it better herself. In essence the proposal aimed to offer a challenging but safe and caring environment to provide disabled children with the opportunity to relax, explore new recreational activities, develop social relationships, foster self-confidence and independence and, above all, to enjoy themselves.

Anna skimmed through a section listing a proposed board of trustees and their objectives. Michael Smith was to be the chairman of the board and the only other name Anna recognised was that of Charlotte Berry. More pages followed on the regulations governing the running of charitable institutions and the permits required for both building and operating

them. Local council regulations pertaining to the pur-
chased block of land were also set out. No major obstacles were predicted.

Anna was very impressed. Mike and his solicitor
had certainly done their homework. Even tentative ar-
chitect and landscape design sketches were included.
Anna smiled at a section in the landscape consultants'
brief. They were to be instructed to consult closely
with both Anna and Nicholas before any designs were
finalised or implemented.

A more personal document followed. Anna's heart-
beat picked up speed as she read the heading of the
contract offering Dr Annalise Van Kessel the position
as director of the proposed holiday camp venture.
Salary and working conditions were to be negotiated
with the chairman of the board, M.G. Smith. The
length of the contract was also negotiable.

A requirement was that Anna's medical training for
the next three years was to be directed towards spe-
cialties of particular relevance to handicapped children. Anna certainly had no problem with that. It was
how she'd have chosen to direct her career in any
case. She was also required to attend relevant medical
conferences accompanied by the chairman of the
board. A proposed list of upcoming events for the
next two years was included. Venues were in London,
Rome, Anaheim, Paris and Geneva.

Anna let out a silent whistle. She wouldn't be complaining of either the travel or the proposed companion. The experience would be immensely rewarding,
both professionally and personally. She almost
laughed out loud at the next condition of employment—that she would live on site and be available at

any time for consultation with the chairman of the trust board.

Anna glanced up as the door of the office opened quietly. Michael Smith took in the sight of the un-wrapped guitar and Anna sitting behind the desk, a sheaf of papers in her hand.

'Have you read it?' he asked.

'Not quite. I'm up to the last bit. It's in very small print.' Anna squinted at the paper.

'It's the fine print.' Mike crossed the room in rapid strides. 'Let me read it to you. It's the most important bit.'

He moved the guitar a little to one side and rested his hip on the desk. Anna handed him the document and he flipped to the last page. For a few seconds he read it silently himself, then he cleared his throat.

'"An agreement is called for between Annalise Van Kessel and Michael George Smith not to impose any unnecessary limitations on any aspect of their future together. They are required to engage in frequent and open communication and to practise the art of compromise whenever appropriate."'

Mike flicked a glance at Anna and then cleared his throat again nervously. He peered at the paper before him as though he was having trouble with the small size of the print.

'"In particular, an acceptable compromise will be negotiated to allow for any conflict between working hours and family commitments should Dr Kessel change her marital status and/or have children in the future."' Mike sighed as though in relief at having expressed a difficult concept. He kept his eyes low-ered and his voice was very quiet as he read out the final clause.

'"Annalise Van Kessel is required to give due consideration to a proposal of marriage by the Chairman of the Board of Trustees, Michael George Smith. The marriage is to be implemented as soon as is practicable should the answer be in the affirmative."'

Mike looked up. The tawny eyes caught and held Anna's shining gaze. 'What do you think?' he queried softly. 'Are you interested in the position?'

'Absolutely.' To Anna's surprise, her voice was confident. It betrayed none of the quivering excitement she felt.

'I don't just mean the job.' Mike's gaze was searching. 'What about the fine print?'

'All of it,' said Anna firmly. 'The fine print and especially the final clause. As far as I'm concerned, it couldn't be any more perfect.'

'Oh, it could be.' Mike's gentle smile faded as he leaned forward to claim Anna's lips with his own. 'And I'll make sure it will be.'

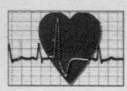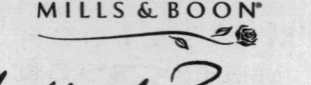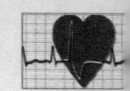

MILLS & BOON®

Medical Romance™

COMING NEXT MONTH from 6th August

ONE IN A MILLION by Margaret Barker
Bundles of Joy

Sister Tessa Grainger remembered Max Forster when he arrived as consultant on her Obs and Gynae ward, for she'd babysat when his daughter Francesca was small. But Max wasn't the carefree man she'd known. Tessa wanted him to laugh again and—maybe—even love again...

POLICE SURGEON by Abigail Gordon

Dr Marcus Owen was happy to be a GP and Police Surgeon, until he found one of the practice partners was Caroline Croft, the woman he'd once loved. Caroline was equally dismayed, for she still loved Marcus! Brought back together by their children, where did they go from here?

IZZIE'S CHOICE by Maggie Kingsley

Sister Isabella Clark came back to discover a new broom A&E consultant, but being followed around by Ben Farrell ended with her speaking her mind and Ben apologised! Since he liked her "honesty", Izzie kept it up, but it wasn't until the hospital fête that they realised they might have something more...

THE HUSBAND SHE NEEDS by Jennifer Taylor
A Country Practice #4

When District Nurse Abbie Fraser hears that Nick Delaney is home, she isn't sure how she feels, for Nick is now in a wheelchair. Surely she can make Nick see he has a future? But at what cost to herself, when she realises she has never stopped loving him?

Available at most branches of WH Smith, Tesco, Asda, Martins, Borders, Easons, Volume One/James Thin and most good paperback bookshops

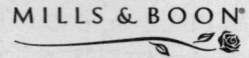

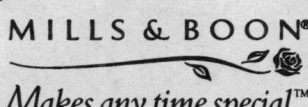

MILLS & BOON®

Makes any time special™

Bestselling themed romances brought back to you by popular demand

Each month By Request brings you three full-length novels in one beautiful volume featuring the best of the best.

So if you missed a favourite Romance the first time around, here is your chance to relive the magic from some of our most popular authors.

**Look out for
Desert Heat in July 1999
featuring Lynne Graham,
Emma Darcy and Sandra Marton**

*Available at most branches of WH Smith, Tesco,
Asda, Martins, Borders, Easons,
Volume One / James Thin
and most good paperback bookshops*

THE Regency COLLECTION

Where rogues find romance

Look out for the fourth volume in this limited collection of Regency Romances from Mills & Boon® in August.

Featuring:

The Outrageous Dowager
by Sarah Westleigh

and

Devil-May-Dare
by Mary Nichols

Still only £4.99

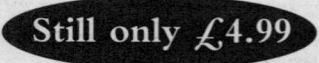

MILLS & BOON®

Makes any time special™

Available at most branches of WH Smith, Tesco, Martins, Borders, Easons, Volume One / James Thin and most good paperback bookshops

2 FREE

books and a surprise gift!

We would like to take this opportunity to thank you for reading this Mills & Boon® book by offering you the chance to take TWO more specially selected titles from the Medical Romance™ series absolutely FREE! We're also making this offer to introduce you to the benefits of the Reader Service™—

- ★ FREE home delivery
- ★ FREE gifts and competitions
- ★ FREE monthly Newsletter
- ★ Exclusive Reader Service discounts
- ★ Books available before they're in the shops

Accepting these FREE books and gift places you under no obligation to buy, you may cancel at any time, even after receiving your free shipment. Simply complete your details below and return the entire page to the address below. *You don't even need a stamp!*

YES! Please send me 2 free Medical Romance books and a surprise gift. I understand that unless you hear from me, I will receive 4 superb new titles every month for just £2.40 each, postage and packing free. I am under no obligation to purchase any books and may cancel my subscription at any time. The free books and gift will be mine to keep in any case.

M9EA

Ms/Mrs/Miss/Mr ....Initials.......................................
BLOCK CAPITALS PLEASE

Surname ....

Address ....

....

....Postcode.................................

Send this whole page to:
THE READER SERVICE, FREEPOST CN81, CROYDON, CR9 3WZ
(Eire readers please send coupon to: P.O. Box 4546, Dublin 24.)